√48

The Merchant of Death

'Have you not seen a pallid face among the crowd . . .
All men must note it, full of horrid dread.'
—Chaucer: 'The Lawyer's Tale'

'In the Middle Ages women doctors continued to
practise in the midst of wars and epidemics as they
always had, for the simple reason that they were needed.'
—Kate Campbellton Hurd-Mead: *A History of Women in Medicine.*

The Merchant of Death

(Being the Third of the Canterbury Tales
of Kathryn Swinbrooke, Leech and
Physician)

C. L. Grace

St. Martin's Press ⚘ New York

THE MERCHANT OF DEATH. Copyright © 1995 by P. C. Doherty.
All rights reserved. Printed in the United States of America. No
part of this book may be used or reproduced in any manner what-
soever without written permission except in the case of brief quo-
tations embodied in critical articles or reviews. For information,
address St. Martin's Press, 175 Fifth Avenue, New York, N.Y.
10010.

Production Editor: David Stanford Burr

Library of Congress Cataloging-in-Publication Data

Grace, C. L.
 The merchant of death / C. L. Grace.
  p. cm.
 ISBN 0-312-13124-0
 1. Great Britain—History—Edward IV, 1461–1483—
Fiction. I. Title.
PR6054.O37M47   1995
823'.914—dc20   95-1741
                                                        CIP

First Edition: June 1995

10 9 8 7 6 5 4 3 2 1

To Grace Harding

Historical Note

In 1471, the bloody civil war between the houses of York and Lancaster was brought to an abrupt end by Edward of York's victories at Barnet and Tewkesbury. The King came into his own and, as autumn turned into winter, sent out his tax collectors to secure what was his.

Now in the fifteenth century, tax collection depended very much on powerful individuals who acted as tax farmers. They were given a fixed amount to raise and what private profits they made were, if they were within reason, ignored by the Crown. Accordingly, fifteenth-century tax collectors were powerful men. Erpingham, the character mentioned here, was a knight, a merchant, and a lawyer. People were as terrified of them as, perhaps, twentieth-century people are of modern taxmen: their powers were quite extensive. Indeed, in the outbreak of every great revolt in English history, be it the Peasants Revolt of 1381 or the English Civil War of the seventeenth century, tax collectors played a vital part!

Prologue

The snow came unexpectedly: thick grey clouds massed over England's east coast, heavy and lowering, as if God himself had turned his hand against the earth. On the octave of the feast of the Immaculate Conception of the Virgin, the snow began to bury the fields and trackways of Kent under thick carpets that hardened into ice. A cold northeasterly wind sprang up and whipped the snow into a fierce blizzard, cutting off hamlets, villages, outlying farms, even placing the King's great city of Canterbury under siege. So heavy did the snow lie upon the turrets, towers and roofs of the cathedral, which housed the bones of the blissful martyr Thomas, that even the great bells could not be rung, lest the iron clappers send the snow hurtling onto the unwary below. Life in Canterbury was reduced to staying indoors and huddling round fires. No trader opened his booth. No tinker, whore or city beadle roamed the streets. Everyone shivered and prayed that the snow would lift by Yuletide and the celebration of Christ's birth.

The monastic chroniclers of Christchurch blew on ice-cold fingers and quietly cursed the blue-green ink freezing in the inkstands. How could they describe these times? The insane and those who saw visions claimed the blizzard was a punishment sent by God because the world stank with the brimstone of hell and the odour of the devil's dung. The scribes liked such phrases and entered their thoughts in the margins of the priory chronicle: how the evil ones now lit black wax candles and, in dark, dank places, seized maidens and imprisoned them in close narrow cells lit by the tallow fat from hanged corpses. If the truth be known, these monkish chroniclers loved to frighten both themselves and their readers, so they imagined another world, a topsy-turvy place in which hares chased dogs and amber-eyed, velvet-skinned panthers fled before deer. Animals with human hands on their backs prowled there as did red-striped dragons, bizarre creatures with serpentine necks twisted into a thousand unbreakable knots. Monkeys with the faces of nuns cavorted in the trees, their furry heads adorned with the horns of stags whilst armless men hunted fish with wings or scaly monsters with lizard snouts. The monkish chroniclers drew these nightmarish drawings to keep themselves amused whilst they stared out of the windows and wondered what this great, cold winter would bring.

At a crossroads miles beyond Canterbury, the Irishman Colum Murtagh, King's Commissioner in Canterbury and Keeper of the King's stables at Kingsmead, was in a nightmare of his own. He wrapped the freezing reins around his hands and stared bleakly across the frozen fields. The dray horses that pulled the cart on which he was sitting snorted in pain from the cold, which froze their hogged manes and clogged their eyes and muzzles. Colum looked despairingly over his shoulder at the provisions stacked in the cart, then turned to the wiry, usually smiling-faced ostler, Henry Frenland, who had accompanied him to the mills at Chilham.

'We should never have left,' Colum murmured. He pointed a finger at the horses. 'They can take little more.'

Colum pulled the cowled hood closer round his head. His ears were freezing and the tip of his nose felt as if some invisible imp had grasped it with ice-cold pincers. Henry Frenland looked mournfully back.

'For God's sake, man!' Colum cursed. 'What is the matter? You have been as miserable as sin since we left Chilham.' He laughed abruptly. 'I know. We are in the wilds of Kent; a blizzard is blowing, we are cut off and lost. Now, what shall we do? Go back or seek refuge at some farm?' He shook his companion. 'Henry!' he exclaimed. 'Are your wits fey? I should have left you at Kingsmead and brought Holbech.'

'All things have their beginning,' Frenland said sonorously as if totally oblivious to the driving snow, freezing cold or Murtagh's questions.

Colum steadied the horses.

'Henry, what is the matter?'

Frenland blinked and stared at Colum.

'I am sorry, Master Murtagh,' he stammered. 'I am truly sorry.'

Colum Murtagh narrowed his eyes. 'How long have you been with me, Frenland?'

'Six months, Master.'

Colum nodded; he stared grimly at the snow-covered scaffold, its gibbet-irons empty, which stood next to the signpost at the crossroads.

'That's right,' he murmured. 'Six months.'

Frenland had been a good servitor, a man gentle with horses, hard-working, industrious, posing no trouble to anyone. No one knew where he came from. However, in the winter months of 1471, with the King's army disbanded after the war against Lancaster, the country lanes were full of former soldiers and landless men seeking work.

'You volunteered to come with me?' Colum asked. 'You are not frightened of the snow?'

Frenland shook his head. 'No, Master, I am not.'

'Well, I am,' Colum replied. 'I don't know where on God's earth we are; I'm freezing cold and the horses won't take much more of this.'

As if to echo his fears the grey-white stillness was broken by a long-drawn-out howl.

'A wolf,' Frenland ventured.

Colum gripped the reins to hide his own fears.

'That's no bloody wolf!' he hissed. 'They are wild dogs, Henry.'

More howls shattered the silence.

'They are hunting in packs,' Colum said. 'Mastiffs, more pow-

3

erful than a wolf, strong as a bear. Animals who used to follow the armies, strays from farms pillaged during the civil war. They have now formed into packs, more dangerous than wolves. Come on!' Colum clicked his tongue at the horses. 'Cheer up, Henry. Have I ever told you the story about the fat abbot, the young maid, a pair of rosy-red lips and lily-white hands?' He started as Frenland gripped the reins.

'Master, I am sorry.'

'What, in God's name . . . !'

Frenland jumped down from the cart and spread his hands. 'Master Murtagh, I am so sorry.'

'For God's sake, stop saying that!' Colum roared. 'What are you sorry about?'

Frenland began to back away. Colum just gaped in astonishment as the groom turned and began to run, stumbling and slipping on the snow back along the trackway.

'Henry!' he shouted. 'Come back! For the love of God, man, you'll die!'

Colum cursed as Frenland disappeared, hidden by the driving snow whilst, to his right, Colum heard the baying of the dogs.

'I can't go after him,' Colum muttered. 'I've got to find shelter.' And, shaking the reins, he urged the great dray horses forward.

The snow was falling thicker. Colum, freezing, stared up at the sky; before him the cobbled track was quickly disappearing under the falling snow and the onset of evening whilst the howls of the dogs drew closer and closer.

Chapter 1

In her house on Ottemelle Lane, Kathryn Swinbrooke, city physician, was also concerned about the snow, which had fallen all night and was now beginning to slide down the red-tiled roof of her house.

'Thomasina,' she called, going to the kitchen door. 'Thomasina, be careful!'

'Don't worry,' her old nurse replied from the garden. 'It will take more than a fall of snow to frighten me.'

Kathryn heard a crash as more snow collapsed, followed by a juicy curse from Thomasina.

'Don't tempt God, Thomasina!' Kathryn warned and stared out at the wild, white wilderness of what was once her garden: now all the herb banks and flower beds, even the stew pond, were blanketed by icy snow. The little benches were almost hidden whilst the two flowered arbours had been turned into white-coated tabernacles.

'Thomasina, what are you doing?' Kathryn's voice rose, alarmed as a great pile of snow fell off the eaves.

'The water butt's frozen solid,' Thomasina shouted back.

Kathryn closed her eyes and prayed for patience. Thomasina was taking out her pent-up fury, hammering the ice until it broke and sloshed in the huge, iron-hooped water cask. Kathryn walked back into the kitchen. The floor rushes were turning black and soggy so she hitched up her woollen gown and began to help her maid Agnes collect them, then carry them out into the garden.

'Why don't I just throw them into the street?' Agnes's bright eyes stared at Kathryn. 'Everyone else does.'

Kathryn finished tying a bundle of rushes together. She shook her head. 'No, Agnes, the streets are clogged and the rushes make good compost for the garden. The snow will soak and rot them.' She smiled. 'And in the spring the flowers and herbs will be that little bit sweeter and stronger.'

Thomasina strode into the kitchen, her fat, friendly face red and sweaty after her exertions.

'Bloody snow!' she muttered. 'Bloody water!' She looked at the rushes being piled high. 'And where's that bloody Irishman? He should be here helping us clean the house. He lives here, doesn't he?'

Kathryn picked up the bundle of rushes and grinned. 'Colum Murtagh is our guest and our friend, Thomasina,' she replied. 'And don't pretend you're angry. You are as worried as I am.'

Thomasina crouched down and began to help Agnes with another pile of rushes.

'He's a fool,' Thomasina groused. 'He should have been back in Kingsmead yesterday. The snow is still falling.' She looked up, her face now worried. 'You've heard the rumours from Rawnose about the packs of wild dogs roaming the Weald of Kent?'

'Those idle buggers, the King's verderers!' Thomasina said.

'Don't swear, Thomasina,' Agnes cried reprovingly, echoing her mistress's usual stricture at Thomasina's profanity.

'Those idle buggers, the King's verderers,' Thomasina repeated meaningfully, 'should have done their job properly in the autumn and hunted the poor things down. Now they roam as wild as wolves whilst Master Murtagh is out there all by himself.'

'No, Henry Frenland's with him,' Kathryn intervened, reassuring herself as well as everybody else.

Thomasina stood up and wiped her hands on her apron. 'I have been married three times,' she declared, beginning her famous and well-worn speech. 'And I have yet to meet a man with true courage. Master Murtagh's retainers out at Kingsmead are, like the King's verderers, idle buggers!'

Thomasina could have bitten out her tongue. Kathryn's usual serene look had disappeared. The old nurse studied her mistress carefully. Kathryn looked untidy with no wimple or veil to cover her black hair, which was now pulled tightly back behind her head; dark circles ringed her eyes and her usual creamy complexion was pallid and sallow.

'I am sorry,' Thomasina said. 'But yes, Mistress, I am worried for Colum. Why did he go out there?'

Kathryn picked up the sheaves of rushes and took them out to the garden. When she returned, Thomasina whispered to Agnes to continue with the task and went and took her mistress's hand. She stared into Kathryn's grey-green eyes, noting the furrows on her brow and round her mouth.

'When you were small,' Thomasina whispered, 'I told you never to frown. Beautiful people always smile.'

Kathryn forced a grin. 'I am worried, Thomasina. Colum had to go. The provender at the stables had run dangerously low whilst the merchants of Canterbury are charging too high a price.'

'Another band of thieving buggers!' Thomasina grumbled. She squeezed Kathryn's hand. 'But you know the Irishman! He's been in greater danger and thrives on it.' She smiled. 'Most ragged-arsed Irishmen do! He'll be back here before noon cursing and swearing, singing some song or, worse, quoting Chaucer to show he isn't a bog Irishman. Now come on, this place is freezing.'

Under Thomasina's coaxing, Kathryn threw herself into a frenzy of activity. The rushes were collected, bound and placed outside, the floor was swept and scrubbed. A blazing fire soon roared in the hearth; the charcoal braziers, standing in every corner, winked and crackled whilst Thomasina placed burning coals in chafing dishes round the house, carefully capped to prevent fire. Soon the kitchen, the small solarium beyond and Kathryn's writing chancery glowed with warmth, sweet-smelling as summer as Kathryn placed small bags of herbs on hooks above the fire. Little Wuf, the blond-haired foundling whom Kathryn had taken into her home, came roaring downstairs pretending to be a knight; he screamed at Agnes that she be the princess and Thomasina the dragon. He was soon sent packing back to his own room. Agnes began to bake oatmeal cakes and a hot stew so they could break their fast, as Thomasina declared, in a truly Christian way.

Once they had eaten, Kathryn went up to her own chamber to change. She closed the bedroom door behind her and flopped down on the great four-poster bed, pulling the woollen coverlet around her. She propped herself up on her elbow and looked across at the hour candle. She wasn't too sure of the time: the candle had gone out and the grey lowering skies seemed to have shortened the time between night and day whilst the heavy snow-falls had silenced the bells of the cathedral and city churches which marked the hours of the day. Was it noon, she wondered?

'Oh, Irishman,' she whispered. 'Where are you?'

She lay back on her pillow, closed her eyes and thought of the vast wildness of Kent: its great open fields and winding track-ways. For a short while she dozed, tossing and turning, plagued by a wild nightmare of Colum freezing to death in his cart or being attacked and savaged by some rabid, red-eyed hound. She woke an hour later. From the kitchen she could hear the chatter of Agnes and Thomasina. She threw back the coverlet and went to the door, half opened it and listened. Still no sign or sound of Colum. She slipped along the gallery and opened the door to his chamber. Inside it was dark and cold with the window shuttered. Kathryn took a candle, lit it from a brazier and put it back on its iron spigot. She stared round the room. 'A soldier's chamber' she always called it and, despite her offers, that's the way Colum wanted it kept: woollen rugs on the floor, a simple cot bed and an iron-bound coffer, which Colum always kept locked, the keys slung round his neck. On the wall, next to leather saddlebags, hung Colum's great war belt. Kathryn glimpsed this and her stomach lurched.

'You should have taken that,' she whispered.

But then she remembered the crossbow Colum carried and tried to calm her anxieties. She walked across the room which smelt of horse and leather and stared down at the table beside Colum's bed. She picked up the battered wooden statue of the Virgin and Child. Despite its age, the wear and tear of the years, the Virgin's smile was still serene as she stared down at the babe in her arms. Feeling slightly guilty, Kathryn put this back and stared at the colourful Celtic cross hanging from a nail above the bed.

'They are the only things my mother gave me,' Colum had once told her, 'Because they were the only things she had. They have been with me everywhere, Kathryn; in camp or in my chamber when I was the King's marshal.'

Kathryn leaned across, touched the crucifix and closed her eyes.

'Come back safe,' she prayed. 'You stupid Irishman, just come back!'

She walked to the foot of the bed and crouched down beside the coffer. What did Colum keep in there? Kathryn wondered, then smiled as she remembered one of Thomasina's many proverbs: 'Curiosity killed the cat!'

'Aye,' Kathryn murmured. 'And satisfaction made it fat!'

She went back to blow the candle out and glimpsed the roll of parchment next to the leather-covered book on the shelf at the side of the door. Kathryn took the roll of vellum down, undid the red cord and read the cramped writing: Colum's collection of stories of ancient Eire, about Cuculhain, Maeve and the fairy land of Tirnaog. She put it back next to the copy of Chaucer's works which she had bought for Colum as a Midsummer present. Kathryn blew the candle out.

'You're becoming maudlin, Swinbrooke,' she mocked herself. 'The Irishman will come back. He'll start teasing and I'll wish he was away again.'

Kathryn returned briskly to her own chamber where she washed and changed. She heard a rap on the door and quickly slipped on a pair of soft buskins, wondering who would brave the elements to call so early. She quietly prayed it was not some emergency. Then a man's voice rang out.

'Colum!' She hurried out of the room to the top of the stairs only to recognise the mellow tones of Simon Luberon, the pompous but kindly clerk of the city council. She hastily ran down the stairs. Luberon was sitting in front of the fire, his cowl and hood thrown back, his fat fingers stretched out to the flames. He rose as Kathryn entered, his merry, fat face alive with pleasure. Luberon would never admit it, but he had a secret liking, even passion, for this serene, dark-haired physician.

'Kathryn.' He held his hands out, then self-consciously slipped them up the voluminous sleeves of his cloak. 'I had better not touch you,' he laughed, coming forward. 'My hands are freezing.'

Kathryn grabbed him by the shoulders and kissed him lightly on each ice-covered cheek.

'Simon, don't you have any gloves?'

The little clerk shifted from one foot to another.

'I did,' he stammered. 'But I lost them.'

Kathryn went across to the linen cupboard, built into the wall of the kitchen next to the hearth. She returned with a pair of dark blue gloves.

'Simon, take these as a gift. Your hands are about the same size as mine.'

Luberon's face flushed with embarrassment but he quickly accepted, slipping them on, spreading his fingers in admiration.

'Marvellous!' he breathed. 'So warm!'

'A man should always be warm,' Thomasina piped up. 'In house and out of house, if you know what I mean, Master clerk?'

Luberon looked quickly at her. The old nurse stared back in round-eyed innocence.

'Come on, Simon, sit down!' Kathryn waved him back to a chair near the inglenook. Agnes pushed another chair alongside. 'Now,' Kathryn said, 'Thomasina will give you some posset. So, why are you here?'

'Murder,' Luberon replied nonchalantly, loosening the clasps of his cloak. He took this off and threw it over the back of the chair. 'You'd think a freezing winter would cool the rage in men's hearts but it's not the case.'

He paused as Thomasina brought him a pewter cup of wine mixed with herbs. She wrapped this in cloths, took a red-hot poker from the fire and placed it in the cup, not withdrawing it until the sizzling ceased.

'There,' Thomasina murmured, placing the wine carefully in the little clerk's hands. 'Drink that, Master Simon, and you'll feel like dancing round the maypole.'

Luberon sipped it carefully. Kathryn crossed her arms, clenching and unclenching her fingers.

'What is it?' she blurted out. 'What murder, Simon?'

Luberon sniffed appreciatively at the rosemary and thyme that floated on the top of his wine cup.

'Do you know Richard Blunt?'

'Yes, he lives in Reeking Alley behind St. Mildred's Church.' Kathryn recalled the old painter's kindly, sun-burnt face, straggling grey hair, sharp blue eyes and, above all, his skill at bringing scenes to life on the grey walls of the parish church. 'He's not dead, surely?'

Luberon shook his head. 'No, he murdered his wife.'

Kathryn went cold and stared into the fire. 'He married last spring, a trader's daughter, Alisoun.'

'That's right,' Luberon confirmed. 'People called it a May and December marriage. He was thirty years her elder.'

Kathryn rubbed her face as Thomasina and Agnes edged closer to listen avidly to the conversation.

'Alisoun was tall and slender as a willow, pretty-faced and blond,' Kathryn recalled, not adding that Colum had once called her hot-eyed and slack-mouthed. She had known and liked Richard Blunt since childhood but she considered Alisoun spoilt and petulant. 'What happened?'

'Well, Richard came home late last night. He was, as you know, finishing a painting in St. Mildred's Church.' Luberon placed the cup on the hearthstone. 'Now, in Blunt's house, the solarium is not on the ground floor but on the one above. Richard and his son Peter, you know the lad? He's a little simple. He often cleans the plaster before his father executes the painting.'

'Go on!' Thomasina interrupted sharply. 'For God's sake, what happened?'

'I don't really know,' Luberon snapped back. 'Old Blunt came

11

home to find two young men dallying with his wife: a scholar called Nicholas from the Halls of Cambridge and his friend, the clerk Absolon, employed by a corn merchant.' Luberon blinked. 'You know the sort, Mistress Kathryn; to them, every woman is suitable prey and they like nothing better than to place a pair of cuckold's horns on a man's head. Anyway, both young men were in a state of undress and so was Alisoun. At least, that's how we found their corpses.'

'All three of them?' Kathryn exclaimed.

'Aye, God knows what happened. But when Blunt opened the door, he'd already collected his bow and quiver of arrows.' Luberon shrugged. 'It was over in seconds. Nicholas took an arrow full in the throat. Alisoun the same. Absolon tried to open a window and jump out, but Richard's third arrow took him in the back.'

Kathryn forgot all about her own anxieties and put her face in her hands. She could imagine the scene; the comfortable solarium, the flickering flames of the fire, the wine cups and soft laughter. Blunt was a master bowman—and what had Colum once told her? Such an archer could loose at least six arrows in a minute and all of them would find their mark.

'What happened then?'

'Well, Absolon's body fell into the street, almost at the feet of Widow Gumple. She called the watch who arrived to find the other two corpses and Richard sitting quietly in his chair staring into the fire. He made no attempt to deny the crime. Peter, who'd returned late from some errand, was standing beside him, just gazing vacuously around.'

'And where are they now?'

'Well, Peter's still at the house but Richard's in the cells at the guildhall. He'll go before the King's Justices and certainly hang.' Luberon ticked the points off on his stubby fingers. 'The murders were cold-blooded. We have the bodies and we have their killer.'

'How is Richard?' Kathryn asked.

'Oh, he's calm and serene. He has openly confessed and is quite resigned to whatever the law ordains.'

Kathryn thought of Blunt's only son by his first marriage: a tall, slack-jawed, gangling young man.

'And they didn't arrest Peter as an accomplice?'

'Oh no. Widow Gumple distinctly remembers Peter coming along the street after Absolon's body tumbled from the window.'

Thomasina came in and took a stool by the fire. 'If Widow Gumple is involved,' she declared darkly, 'then all of Canterbury will know by noon and all of Kent by tomorrow. She has a clacking tongue, old Gumple!'

Kathryn stared at her nurse curiously. Widow Gumple was a leading member of the parish council, a spiteful chatterbox, pompous and haughty, rather ridiculous in her ornate head-dresses and flouncy gowns. Kathryn often wondered whether there was some secret source for Thomasina's dislike, even hatred, for that foolish old gossip. She glanced at Luberon.

'Simon, this is dreadful news. But what can I do?'

'Ah.' Luberon played with his new gloves. 'The corpses are to be examined and you, Mistress Swinbrooke, are the city physician. I would also be grateful if you'd visit the house. Peter may need some assistance. Finally, Richard Blunt himself has asked to speak to you.'

'Me!' Katryn exclaimed. 'He has not been to see me for at least fourteen months!'

'He still wishes to see you,' Luberon said. He stared round. 'However, that is not the real reason I'm here. Has Master Murtagh returned?'

'No,' Kathryn sighed. 'And we are all beginning to worry about his whereabouts.'

'In which case, Mistress, you must come by yourself. There's been another death.'

Kathryn groaned.

'This one's more official,' Luberon explained. 'You know the tavern, the Wicker Man, just past the castle near Worthingate?'

Kathryn nodded.

'Well, last night that spacious, comfortable place had all its rooms taken up by travellers trapped by the inclement weather.

Amongst these was a royal tax collector, Sir Reginald Erpingham.' Luberon sighed, picked up the cup, drained it and got to his feet. 'To cut a long story short, Mistress, this morning Erpingham was found dead in bed.'

'And the cause?'

Luberon shrugged into his cloak. 'Dead as a nail, the mean-hearted bastard.' He smiled apologetically at Kathryn. 'I am sorry, Mistress, but he was. Erpingham won't be missed, but the hundreds of pounds sterling in royal taxes he was carrying will be.'

'Stolen?' Kathryn exclaimed.

'Gone as if it had never existed. I've just come from there. You'd best see for yourself. Mistress, you have to come!'

Kathryn could see she had no choice. Colum was royal coroner in the city and she had an indenture with the city council as his official physician, with a duty to investigate any mysterious death, particularly the likes of Erpingham.

'I'll come as well,' Thomasina offered, getting to her feet.

'No, Thomasina, stay here!' Kathryn looked around the room. 'By the way, where's Wuf? He's gone very quiet.'

'He's upstairs,' Thomasina said. 'Back at his carving he is.' The old woman's face softened. 'But, Mistress, you must look at it. He does have a gift. Are you sure I shouldn't go with you?'

'No,' Kathryn repeated. 'Now, stop listening to other people's conversations and get my saddlebags down. I need a roll of parchment and a leather pouch with my quills. The tavern will provide me with ink.' She thought of Peter Blunt, terrified out of his wits, and of his father, Richard, locked in some lonely, cold dungeon. 'Oh, and a small jar of balm, a very small pot. Now, Thomasina, if Master Murtagh returns, tell him where we have gone. First to the Wicker Man, then to Blunt's house and on to the guildhall.'

Thomasina reluctantly agreed. She brought a pair of leather boots for Kathryn and a second set of woollen stockings. Kathryn took these and finished dressing in her small chancery office. By the time she returned, Luberon was ready to leave.

'It's not far,' he declared. 'Mistress, you might as well walk—it will be safer.'

Kathryn agreed. She told Thomasina to keep an eye on Wuf and followed Luberon out into the freezing cold. Ottemelle Lane and all the thoroughfares were fairly deserted. The blizzard had stopped but the snow still fell in soft, gentle flakes to lie thick on the sloping roofs or hang out in frozen lumps over the eaves. Luberon and Kathryn had to pick their way carefully because the snow had hidden the sewers as well as the usual rubbish strewn in the streets. They made their way gingerly down the lane, keeping a wary eye on the snow crashing from the roofs onto the streets below. Now and again, the occasional window would be thrown open as maids poured out the contents of night jars to turn the snow in front of the houses into a sloppy, stinking mess. Kathryn gripped Luberon's arm; the clerk preened himself, patting her hand gently.

'Thank you, Kathryn,' he murmured.

'What for?' she asked, puzzled.

Luberon's little red face peered out from the cowl of his hood. 'For the gloves,' he replied. 'And for coming with me.'

'I'll knit you a pair myself,' Kathryn said. 'Simon, it's time you found a good woman.'

'Like Thomasina?' Luberon teased back.

'Thomasina may be too much of a handful,' Kathryn laughed.

They paused at the corner of Ottemelle Lane. Some kindly burgess had stacked a pile of logs and lit a fire in the middle of the thoroughfare for the beggars and poor of the city to get some warmth. These, garbed in rags from head to toe, were now gathered round the bonfire murmuring and jostling one another. Kathryn's stomach turned at the foul smell of burning fat as beggars tried to cook the pieces of meat they had managed to filch or beg. Near the bonfire, lying on its side, was a thin-ribbed dog, its mangy carcase frozen hard. Two urchins were dancing round it, poking it with a stick. Kathryn fished into her purse, tugging at Luberon's arm so he would stop. She held up a coin.

'Leave it alone!' she said to the thin-faced waifs. 'Here, come with me!'

They grasped the coin and followed Kathryn and Luberon as they turned into Hethenman Lane.

'See,' Kathryn declared, pointing to the line of people outside the baker's shop. 'Ask Master Bernard. Say Mistress Swinbrooke.' She made the children repeat the name. 'Say Mistress Swinbrooke wants you to have some hot ginger.'

The two children scampered off.

'We'll have to do something,' Luberon mumbled. 'Those bloody monks at the monastery could be of more help. Canterbury is full of beggars and some of them will not live to see spring.'

Two debtors released from the town gaol, manacled together at wrist and ankle, shuffled towards them, hands extended, begging for alms for themselves and other inmates. Kathryn and Luberon gave each of them a coin.

'It's always the same,' Kathryn murmured. 'The heavy snow hides the disease in the city but those who can't cope become more than obvious.'

She stared round. Apart from the bakery, all the other shops were shut; the stalls and booths stood empty, and the houses were closed and shuttered against the freezing cold. Not even children played. Kathryn had to stop now and again to stamp her feet to keep warm. At last, they turned down Worthingate Lane, which ran under the towering mass of Canterbury Castle, and, just past Winchepe Gate, entered the spacious, cobbled yard of the Wicker Man tavern. Kathryn heaved a sigh of relief: the yard around the tavern had been cleared of snow and strewn with a mixture of salt and soil to prevent people slipping. When a young lad came up to enquire their business, Luberon tartly announced who he was as Kathryn stared round. The Wicker Man was a wealthy, prosperous place well situated between the fields and the city. Its outside walls were dressed with grey ragstone, the cobbles were smooth and neatly laid, and the stables and outhouses looked well kept with their woodwork clean and freshly painted. Kathryn caught the fragrant smell of cooking coming from the kitchens. She looked up and noticed how, on the top storey, the windows were mere arrow slits but, on the ground and first floors, the windows were broad and filled with lead and painted glass. The lad led them into the empty, whitewashed kitchen, eerie in its silence. No ovens burned except the small bakery next to the hearth, the source of the delicious smell of cooking. The tables and ledges were so clean even Thomasina would approve of their scrubbed surfaces, whilst the tankards, pots, basins and ewers gleamed on the shelves round the room.

'I told them not to touch anything,' Luberon declared pompously as they left the kitchen and went down a sandstone passage into the great taproom. A number of people stood there: the blacksmith, ostlers, grooms in grubby, straw-colored raiment and the cooks and scullions in their stained aprons. Luberon ignored these and went across to the group sitting around a polished oval table in the window embrasure. They stopped chattering as Luberon approached and stared blankly at the clerk, then just as coldly at Kathryn.

'So, you have returned at last?' one man asked.

'Yes, yes, I have. This is Mistress Swinbrooke, physician in the city.'

'Where's the coroner?' the same man asked.

'He'll be along soon,' Kathryn replied. 'And who, sir, are you?'

'Tobias Smithler, landlord.'

Kathryn stared at this thin pikestaff of a man with his mop of sandy-red hair. Smithler was hard-eyed, his nose as bent as a falcon's, with a mouth that seemed to run like a slit from ear to ear. He was soberly dressed in dark blue fustian and made no attempt to hide his hostility to both Luberon and Kathryn. Luberon ignored the landlord's bad manners as he introduced the rest of the company: Smithler's wife, Blanche, modestly dressed in a bottle-green dress, tied high at the neck. She was petite, her features well formed, her lips generous and eyes full of merriment. Kathryn thought how ill-matched the pair were and quietly wondered if the landlord spent a great deal of his time making sure the guests did not think the tavern's hospitality extended to embracing his wife. Kathryn immediately felt guilty at her uncharitableness; Blanche was simply trying to make up for her husband's bad manners. She was eager to please and clearly nervous, constantly plucking at the cord tied round her slim waist.

Kathryn smiled reassuringly at her but her boorish husband was not easily ignored.

'What?' he exclaimed, pointing at Kathryn, then paused at a sound from the kitchen. 'What?' he repeated, 'is she doing here?'

'I have explained that,' Luberon replied patiently, drawing himself up to his full height and puffing out his pigeon chest.

'Yes, and I have been waiting,' Smithler snapped. 'I have a tavern to run, Master clerk. I am sorry Erpingham's dead but I have meals to cook.' He glared round at the rest of the group. 'Rooms to be cleaned and I'd like that bloody corpse removed!'

Kathryn quietly groaned at the look of obstinate malice on the tavern-keeper's face.

'Master Smithler,' she began. 'I . . .' She saw the expression on the fellow's face abruptly fade as he stared over her shoulder.

'You'll do what you are bloody well told!' a voice exclaimed behind her.

Kathryn whirled round. 'Colum!'

The Irishman stood there, hair unkempt, face unshaven, swathed in his thick brown military cloak. Nevertheless, she could understand why Smithler had become cautious: Colum, despite his shabby appearance, exuded both menace and authority. Kathryn felt like running towards him and throwing her arms round his neck, but the look in Colum's eyes and the slight shake of his head warned her against any show of emotion. Instead, he walked forward and quietly squeezed her by the arm.

'Master Luberon.' He smiled down at the clerk, only too grateful for Colum's intervention. 'I have been away on business.' He glanced sideways at Kathryn and grinned. 'A small matter. It delayed me longer than I thought.' He undid the cords of his cloak and threw it at Smithler. 'And, before you ask, my name is Colum Murtagh, the King's own Commissioner in Canterbury. Now, sir, hang that up! I need a goblet of wine, some victuals then I want to know what this is all about!'

Chapter 2

Whilst Smithler served Colum fresh manchet loaves, cheese and salted strips of bacon, Luberon introduced the rest of the company. Miles Stanton was the royal serjeant in charge of Erpingham's escort; he was dressed in a leather jerkin and leggings, his hair cropped so close Kathryn at first thought he was bald. A professional soldier, Standon looked dour with the grim face of a hardened killer. He knew full well that the blame for Erpingham's murder would be laid at his door and he would be held accountable. He indicated with one hand to the far end of the tavern where the rest of his small escort sat. Kathryn peered over her shoulder at them, trying to ignore Colum's secret smile and hidden wink.

'A fine group,' Colum murmured.

Kathryn caught the sarcasm in his voice. The soldiers were grizzled veterans who looked as if they would burn a widow's hovel just for the fun of it. Next to Standon sat Eudo Vavasour, a little mouse of a man, grey-garbed, grey-haired, grey-faced with frightened eyes and a nose that would never stop twitching. Kathryn had to bite her own lips to stop herself smiling at his nervousness. The next person had no humour about him: Sir Gervase Percy sat as far away from the rest as he could. Whilst Luberon grandly introduced him, Kathryn tried to ignore Colum's gaze. She would have loved to have screamed at the Irishman, 'Where have you been?' and 'Why have you caused us so much heartache?' But she quietly vowed she would deal with such matters later. Instead she studied this self-styled grand old man. A distant member of the powerful Percy family, Sir Gervase had a nut-brown face. He was dressed in dark brown fustian; his jerkin was of pure wool; he wore a fine linen shirt, and the rings on his fingers were studded with jewels the size of small pebbles. An imperious knight, he kept upright by leaning on the hilt of his sword. Behind the knight sat a black-garbed priest, Father Eal-dred. He was quiet-spoken with a pallid, ascetic face and Kathryn wondered what he was doing in Canterbury so far from his parish. A loving couple were the last guests. Alan de Murville was tall, dark and well-favoured, a lord who owned lush meadows and fertile fields around Rochester. Margaret, his wife, was blond, slender as a willow, with the soft, gentle eyes and manners of a baby fawn.

Once the introductions were made, Luberon coughed and tapped on the table.

'A crime has been committed!' he trumpeted. 'A grievous felony against our King, Edward IV, God bless him! One of his officials, Sir Reginald Erpingham, has been found dead and his money, the Crown's own taxes, stolen. The culprit must be in this room.' Luberon paused for effect. 'I now ask you all, each on his or her allegiance, do you know anything about this dreadful crime?'

Except for a slight whimper from Vavasour, there was no reply.

'In which case,' Colum got to his feet, scratching his unshaven cheek, 'I must ask all of you to stay here till I and Mistress Swinbrooke have pursued these matters to a satisfactory conclusion.'

The Irishman stared round the spacious taproom. No one dared object, though the landlord looked daggers at Kathryn and a general hubbub broke out amongst the servants who stood near the beer barrels and wine vats.

'We have our tasks to do!' one of them wailed. 'We cannot stay here all day!'

The protest grew into a chorus. Tobias Smithler, encouraged by these, took a step forward.

'Master Murtagh,' he insisted. 'I have a tavern, a hostelry to run. Surely my servants can go about their duties?'

'Of course.' Murtagh beamed across at the servants. 'You may do as you wish.' He turned to Luberon. 'Master Simon, you will, however, instruct the servants not to leave.' He pointed at the royal serjeant. 'Master Standon, your men will guard all doors and any other entrances.' Colum pulled a face and winked at Kathryn. 'Mistress Swinbrooke, we should view the corpse.'

Led by a surly-looking Smithler, Kathryn and Colum Murtagh made their way to the stairs. As Luberon waddled off in front of them, Kathryn immediately grabbed Colum by his sleeve, pulling him back.

'Where in God's name have you been, Irishman? We have all been worried sick!'

Colum scratched his black, curly hair and grinned lazily down at her.

'Did you miss me, Kathryn?' he whispered. 'Did you really miss me so much?'

'We all missed you.'

Colum, despite his tiredness and grubby appearance, had the devil's own mischief in him. He shrugged, leaned down and whispered in her ear.

'Well, Mistress Swinbrooke, until you tell me that you really missed me, I shan't tell you where I have been. And only the good Lord knows'—he hitched his cloak around him—'how many sweet distractions lurk along the road to Canterbury!'

Kathryn's reply was to kick him sharply on the ankle and follow Smithler and Luberon through the taproom door and into the stone-flagged passageway towards the stairs.

'Master Smithler,' Kathryn called, her cheeks still burning after her encounter with Colum. 'On which floor was Sir Reginald?'

'There are two more floors,' the landlord replied. 'Sir Reginald was on the first, the top floor is used for the servants and scullions.' Smithler leaned against the balustrade and stared down at Colum, totally ignoring Kathryn. 'This hostelry is rather like any great town house, built in the form of a square.' He tapped the newel post. 'But served by one staircase. On each floor are corridors with four chambers on each. Sir Reginald always stayed in the end chamber on the gallery to the right.' Smithler shrugged. 'We call it the Haunted Room.'

'Why is that?' Luberon asked.

Smithler looked up at the blackened beams. 'This is an old tavern. There was a hostelry here long before Becket was murdered in his cathedral: three, four hundred years old, though it was rebuilt in the time of King John after the great fire which swept through Worthingate.'

'And the ghost story?' Colum insisted, always intrigued by such matters. 'Why is the room haunted?'

'They say a murder occurred,' Smithler replied. 'Many years ago.' He smiled thinly. 'A priest eloped with some noble-born lady. She repented because she was destined for a nunnery. In a fit of rage he is supposed to have killed her and fled.' Smithler raised his eyebrows. 'I don't know the real truth of it. Some guests claim to see apparitions and hear the sound of weeping but I never have.'

'Sir Reginald did!' a harsh voice behind them snapped.

Kathryn turned around. Sir Gervase stood there leaning on his sword. He tapped this against the stone floor. 'Sir Reginald said he saw a ghost the night before he died.'

'Oh, don't be stupid!' Smithler replied. 'Sir Reginald had probably drunk too much, which is true of a few other people in this tavern!'

The old man refused to be cowed and shook his head defiantly. 'Watch your tongue! Two nights ago Sir Reginald woke up screaming. I know. He pounded on my door and woke me up. Bathed in sweat he was, face as white as his nightshirt. I had to take him into my own chamber to calm him down, he was so terrified.'

'What did he claim to have seen?' Luberon asked.

'He said he saw a ghost: a woman dressed in a white shroud, pale-faced and red-eyed.' Sir Gervase shook his head. 'Sir Reginald was fair afright. He had been sick; his mouth was all stained and when I took him back to his room, the place smelt sour.'

'Sir Reginald was sick all right,' Smithler interrupted. 'The scullion who had to empty his night jar complained of the filth.'

'And yesterday?' Kathryn asked.

Sir Gervase was now thoroughly enjoying being the centre of attention.

'Erpingham looked a bit pale at breakfast. But,' he shrugged. 'we were all locked in because of the snow. By noon he was eating heartily enough and not rushing to the latrines. He made no more reference to the ghost. Sir Reginald,' Sir Gervase concluded, 'did not have the sweetest temperament. I was very wary of him so I let the matter rest.'

'Enough of this,' Colum intervened. 'Sir Reginald's sickness, be it of the mind or the body, can wait. Master taverner, let's view the corpse.'

Smithler led them up the steep stairway to two huge timbered pillars at the top. The galleries running to the left and right of these were unremarkable: the walls were clean and whitewashed, the woodwork smartly painted black. Kathryn looked down the galleries. Four chambers stood on each, their doors huge, heavy-set and reinforced with iron studs. Smithler led them down the gallery on the right. The end room, Sir Reginald's, was in utter disarray. The floor outside was gouged and the door, smashed off its leather hinges, stood crookedly against the lintel. Smithler, with the help of Colum, pushed it gently to one side and led them in. Kathryn shivered and the hair on the nape of her neck curled. The place smelt sour and it had been a long time since Kathryn had felt such a sense of dread with the hand of death so close.

Tobias lit a rushlight on the wall, then a candle on the table. Kathryn gazed at Colum and Luberon. They, too, were uneasy even though nothing was amiss in the room. It was a perfect square, the ceiling of ribbed design, the black timber beams contrasting sharply with the white plaster. The walls were lime-washed and draped with canvas or linen cloths. The rushes on the wooden floor were clean, dry and sprinkled with fresh herbs. A small cupboard stood in one corner and, at the base of the great four-poster bed, a large wooden chest. Beside this lay two leather panniers or saddlebags, their clasps undone, the covers thrown back to reveal a pile of stones.

'The tax money was in them?' Kathryn asked.

Smithler shrugged. 'That's what Standon said.'

'And I was right.' The royal serjeant came in uninvited. Behind him, in the gallery, stood the landlord's wife, her pretty face drawn and anxious. Colum opened his mouth to tell Standon to leave but he caught Kathryn's warning glance.

'Well, let's see him!' Colum growled, gesturing at the bed curtains.

Luberon pulled these back. Sir Reginald Erpingham lay there, covered by a sheet. Kathryn slowly lifted it back and stared down at the dead tax collector: a small, thickset man, balding head, fleshy featured, his eyes tightly closed, the lids held down by two pennies. Kathryn leant down and sniffed at the lips, then felt the man's hands, cold and hardening.

'What time was he discovered dead?' she asked.

'Early this morning,' Smithler replied.

'And what time did you retire last night?' Kathryn now slipped her hand beneath the dead man's nightshirt, pressing his chest and stomach.

'About eight o'clock.'

Kathryn shook her head. 'Well, he's been dead for hours,' she muttered. 'The flesh feels waxy, the bones and muscles hardening.' She peered closer. 'Colum, pull back the bed drapes. Master Standon, open the window. No, stop!'

She walked towards the window. 'On second thought I'll open it myself.'

Kathryn carefully lifted the latch on the shutters and pulled them back. She stared closely at the latch on the window casement; she then pressed this down and pushed it open, knocking the snow off the ledge into the yard below.

Colum came up behind her. 'What's the matter, Kathryn?'

'I am not speaking to you, Irishman,' she whispered. 'You owe me an explanation.' She turned away. 'I think Erpingham was murdered,' she declared. 'I just want to make sure this window hadn't been forced.'

The landlord quickly understood what Kathryn was doing.

'Mistress Swinbrooke, that window has not been open for at least a week.'

'I can see that,' Kathryn replied, coming back to the bed and staring down at the corpse, which now looked ghastly in the poor light coming through the open casement. She lifted up the heavy nightshirt and stared down at the greyish-white flesh, the rather shrivelled testicles and the flabby chest, stomach and thighs.

'Not the prettiest of sights,' Standon muttered.

They all grouped round the bed. Kathryn glimpsed a small goblet of wine on the table. She picked this up and sniffed. It only contained a few dregs of wine and smelt untainted. Kathryn carefully dipped her finger in and licked.

'Was that safe?' Colum murmured.

'Yes, it's only wine.' She stared across at Smithler. 'The tax collector took this up on the night he retired?'

'Oh, yes, nothing has been touched. Master Luberon ordered that.'

Now Luberon took the goblet; he swilled the wine round, noticing the thin coating on the top, how deeply stained the pewter cup was.

'Yes, that's the cup I saw when I came here this morning,' he declared. 'And the wine's been in it for some time. Mistress Swinbrooke, what is the matter?'

Kathryn once more sniffed the dead man's slightly stained mouth, pulled back the eyelids and ran her hand over the swollen stomach.

'Colum, bring a candle closer.'

The Irishman obeyed.

'Closer still!' she urged. 'Near the face!'

Colum did so and gasped as he noticed the faint red blotches, like scabs on the man's cheeks. The same reddish marks covered the corpse's throat, chest and stomach.

'What is it?'

'Sir Reginald Erpingham,' Kathryn replied, sitting on the edge of the bed, 'did not die of a seizure or apoplexy, or from any natural cause. He died from the commonest and most virulent of poisons. What the Latinists would call belladonna or the common tongue deadly nightshade.' She pointed to the flushed skin and then gingerly put her finger between the man's lips. 'All the signs are here. First, his mouth reeks of it. You see, deadly nightshade is a tall perennial herb and can be gathered from any wood, thicket or hedgerow. The purple bell flower is nothing, but its leaves and roots hold a deadly potion. After death the symptoms become quite apparent: the abdomen slightly swollen, the skin flushed in places, particularly the face and neck, which become waxlike to the touch. The dead man's lips and mouth are as dry as sand and his pupils remain widened.'

She got to her feet and carefully covered the naked corpse. 'Sir Reginald Erpingham was poisoned. Death would have come very quickly.' She shrugged. 'It would occur well within half an hour.'

'Wouldn't he have known?' Colum asked. 'And struggled against it or cried for help?'

Kathryn shook her head. 'No, the symptoms are very similar to those of a sudden seizure.'

She stared round the chamber. Apart from the open window and the saddlebags, everything seemed in place. The small fire that had burned in the hearth was now a pile of white ash. In the far corner lay a heap of the dead man's clothing: jerkin, tunic, hose and war belt. Kathryn pointed at them.

'Is this how they were this morning?'

'Oh, yes,' Standon replied. 'Why?'

Kathryn gestured at a peg driven into the wall. 'I was just curious. Why didn't he hang them up there?'

Standon muttered something about Erpingham being an untidy bastard which Kathryn chose to ignore. She walked across and studied the pile of clothing.

'How was Erpingham discovered?' Colum asked.

'Well, I came up this morning.' Standon replied. 'I knocked and knocked. I knew something had happened so I called Smithler and'—Standon sighed noisily—'he told me to piss off, he was too busy in the kitchen. He did allow Vavasour and some of my soldiers to use a bench and we knocked the door clean off its hinges.'

Kathryn went and studied the door very carefully. She tapped the key.

'And this was still in the lock?'

'Yes,' Standon replied. 'Both Vavasour and I checked that; it was also bolted.'

Now Colum sauntered across and carefully checked the bolts, recalling how, only a few months earlier at the castle, a door that was supposed to be bolted had, in fact, simply been locked from the outside. But this time there could be no mistake: the bolts and the clasps had been torn away, the metal bending. The wood on both the door and lintel had roughly splintered and the lock was bent.

'This door was forced all right,' he said.

'So?' The Irishman pointed down at the corpse. 'What else did you discover?'

Standon shrugged. 'What you see. The window was secured. The fire dead.'

Colum went over and stood under the lintel of the door and stared up curiously.

'This is crooked,' he exclaimed and then went out to the gallery before coming back in. 'All the door lintels are slightly crooked. Why is that?'

'This is an old building,' Smithler replied. 'Foundations are strong but wood moves.' He smiled thinly. 'Which is why every door creaks on its leather hinges.'

Kathryn meanwhile had walked back to the saddlebags.

'These were open?' she asked.

'No,' Standon replied. 'The bags were clasped but when we opened them we found nothing but stones and rocks.'

'How much was there?' Colum said.

'I don't know,' the soldier stammered, his face paling. 'But Vavasour murmured something about two hundred and fifty pounds sterling in good coin.'

Colum whistled under his breath and stared at Kathryn.

'The King will be furious,' Standon muttered. 'If the money

was in coin, its market value was probably worth much more, perhaps even as high as four hundred pounds.'

'And where had it been collected from?' Colum insisted.

'Until the roads closed,' Standon said, 'from the villages between Rochester and Canterbury.' He looked hard-eyed at Kathryn. 'And, before you say it, Mistress, I know what you are thinking.'

'What?' she asked innocently.

The soldier looked down at the floor and nervously tugged at his belt. 'There is no guarantee that the silver hadn't gone missing before Erpingham was murdered or even before he arrived here.'

'Yes,' Kathryn replied softly. 'I had thought of that.'

'So.' Colum walked over and kicked the saddlebag with the toe of his boot. 'I think it was here when Erpingham retired last night. He brought up a cup of wine, which, we now know, contained no trace of poison. He locked and bolted the door; the saddlebags, we can only surmise, were secure, the windows both closed and shuttered. In the morning, however, Erpingham was found poisoned. Neither the door nor window had been interfered with and there is no trace of poison in the room, yet Erpingham is dead and the King's taxes gone.' Colum shrugged. 'There must only be one conclusion: someone came at night through a secret passageway in and out of this room and poisoned Erpingham.'

'But that can't be,' Standon objected. 'After the meal, I slept in the gallery. Mistress Smithler gave me a mattress and a blanket. I always slept near Sir Reginald's room. Moreover, as the landlord says, these doors creak when they open. Neither I, nor Sir Gervase asleep in the adjoining chamber, heard any disturbance.'

'And there are no secret passageways,' Smithler intervened. 'I assure you of that, Master Murtagh.' He shrugged. 'If you wish, you can make your own investigation.'

Kathryn crossed her arms and stared round this bleak chamber. Why, she wondered, was it so oppressive, so evil? What danger, what menace lurked here? She recalled her father's words, Physician Swinbrooke, who now lay coffined beneath the slabs in St. Mildred's Church. *'Never be fearful of the dead, Kathryn. Whatever you see, whatever you hear, whatever you feel, the dead are with God. If you must, only fear the living.'* Kathryn drew in her breath sharply.

'Master Simon.' She glanced at Luberon, who was also standing uneasily, shuffling from foot to foot. 'You were called here this morning?'

The little clerk nodded. 'Yes, Standon immediately sent a messenger to the guildhall.'

'And I stood on guard,' the serjeant said. 'Until he arrived. The landlord and the rest came in but nothing in this room was disturbed.'

Kathryn looked at the little clerk.

'Is that right, Master Simon?'

Luberon nodded.

'In which case,' Kathryn continued, 'let us return to the taproom. Master Smithler,' she smiled placatingly. 'I have walked through the cold and snow. My feet are freezing, my stomach is empty. I would appreciate some hot food.'

'Who will pay for it?' Smithler demanded crossly.

'I will,' Luberon replied. 'Whatever is bought here on the King's business, send your bills in to the guildhall with any receipts. Mistress Swinbrooke, what else?'

'After we have eaten, and perhaps the rest could join us, I need to speak to all the other guests. You'd agree, Master Murtagh?'

The Irishman, who was sitting on the bed, eyes heavy, suddenly stirred.

'Of course. Now leave us for a while.'

Kathryn stood back and waited for the rest to leave.

'What a pretty mess,' Colum muttered. He got up, making sure the corpse was covered from head to toe by pulling the bedclothes up over it. 'Kathryn, this is not guildhall business but the King's. He'll want an answer from me, Erpingham's murderer caught and, above all, that money returned.'

'And I want an answer from you,' Kathryn said, turning to face him. 'Irishman, you are over a day late. You go wandering off across the Weald of Kent. A sudden snowstorm blows in and you disappear. Then you come striding back as if you had been playing with the ducks on the River Stour.'

Colum smiled mischievously, enjoying the sparks in Kathryn's eye and the colour high in her cheek. He looked at Kathryn's black hair, slightly greying at the temples, peeping out from beneath her veil: her eyes and her body tense, her pretty chin now slightly up, hands clenched together.

'So, you did miss me, Kathryn?'

'If you say that again,' she replied, 'I'll pick something up and, this time, I won't miss you, Irishman!'

Colum opened his mouth to tease her but he saw the warning look in Kathryn's eyes. Normally placid and serene, Kathryn had a hot temper and a biting tongue to match. He strode over and grasped her hands.

'Now, now, listen, Kathryn. I left Chilham—'

Kathryn pulled her hands away. 'I gather that.'

'At a crossroads outside the village,' Colum continued. 'Frenland, the ostler who came with me, suddenly got down from the cart and ran away.'

Kathryn's mouth opened in astonishment.

'You mean, he just climbed off the cart and disappeared in the middle of a snow-swept countryside?'

Colum nodded. 'I know, Kathryn.' He shook his head. 'The man must have been witless or he just panicked. I have seen that happen before: seven years ago at the battle of Towton, some of the King's troops were more frightened of the blizzard than they were of the enemy.'

'But you said he was a steady man?'

'As Chaucer says,' Colum replied, ' "I have seen madness laughing in his rage." Anything is possible.'

' "Your wit is thin",' Kathryn snapped back.

'Who said that?' Colum asked.

'Read your Chaucer,' Kathryn replied. 'The Merchant's Tale. Colum, you have lost one of your men, people will ask questions. I remember Frenland, he was small, black-haired; didn't he have a wife out at Kingsmead?'

Colum nodded. 'I have to tell her yet.'

'What happened then?' Kathryn asked.

'I drove the cart on,' Colum replied. 'Night was coming, the blizzard was growing fiercer and, all around me, I could hear the howling of those wild dogs. God knows how I did it and God bless the brave hearts of those horses. I reached a farmstead where I spent the night. The farmer was an honest man. I hired a sturdy garron and made my way back. I didn't bother to go to Kingsmead but came straight to Ottemelle Lane. Thomasina told me about Luberon's visit, the murder of the painter's wife as well as this sorry mess.' He stared across at the corpse lying on the bed, then smiled back at Kathryn. 'We are never alone in a room are we, Mistress Swinbrooke?'

'No.' Kathryn came over, grasped his hands and stared up straight into his heavy-lidded eyes. 'Thomasina was right.' She said, touching the stubble on his dirty cheek. 'Never trust a sweet-talking, bog-trotting Irishman. I am glad you are back, Colum, I was worried sick.' She let go of his hand but nipped his knuckle. 'No questions, Colum, about whether I missed you or not. You know my state: I am married to Alexander Wyville, though God knows where he is! Now, that I can come to terms with.' She winked at the Irishman. 'But if anything happened to you, bog-trotter'—Kathryn touched her chest—'something in here would die and never come back to life.'

Colum was tempted to question her further but Luberon suddenly appeared in the doorway.

'They are all assembled, Mistress Kathryn. Mistress Smithler has something fragrant in the pot.' He stepped round the broken door and walked into the room. 'Is it me?' he asked. 'Or is there something about this chamber? Something of the sepulchre, the touch of death?' He pointed at Colum. 'Are you fey, Irishman? Can't you sense something?'

Colum pulled a face. 'Earlier this year,' he replied, 'I took part in the King's victory at Tewkesbury. Near a ford across the Severn, the Lancastrian dead were piled waist high. Now, there I could smell and taste death.'

'Wait!' Kathryn walked across and pointed at the wall. 'Look, there's a painting, very faded.'

They crossed over and watched as Kathryn's finger traced the outlines of a faded painting.

'Done years ago,' Kathryn declared. 'In red, black and green. Two figures. Look, there's the outline of a priest kneeling, and here is a woman's wimple and dress.' She pointed to a dark shape with black horns on a goatlike head.

'The Lord Satan,' Colum replied. 'Perhaps you are right, Master Luberon.' He pushed aside the rushes and started tapping the floor. 'Perhaps this is some hell chamber. If necessary, I'll pull it to pieces bit by bit to discover the mystery.' He kicked the saddlebag full of rocks. 'I have seen the best counterfeit men ply their trade at fairs and markets, but you'd need the devil's skill to murder a man in a locked room, take his treasure and replace it with stones without leaving the slightest trace of your felony.' Colum went and stared out of the window. 'Thank God I haven't had to report this immediately to the King.' He closed the shutters with a bang. 'However, there's a thaw on its way.'

'How can you tell that?' Kathryn asked.

Colum winked and knowingly tapped the side of his nose. Luberon looked away, embarrassed and slightly jealous. He liked the Irishman but he adored Mistress Swinbrooke. Luberon recalled her words about meeting some good woman. I have met her, Luberon realised, staring sadly at Kathryn, but God knows I can never tell her.

'Come on,' Kathryn murmured. 'Let's not keep Master Smithler's profits from suffering too much.'

They went out into the gallery where they could hear the hubbub from the taproom below. Kathryn glimpsed the capped wooden buckets standing along the gallery.

'Against fire,' Luberon declared, following her glance. He puffed his chest out and pulled his shoulders back. 'City regulations demand at least three buckets of water on each gallery in any tavern.'

Colum slapped him on the back. 'Come on, Master Luberon, my belly thinks my throat's been cut!'

They went down to the taproom where the Smithlers' servants and scullions were serving a fragrant dish in pewter bowls with fresh manchet loaves wrapped in napkins. The rest of the guests ignored them as they took their seats near the roaring fire. Kathryn picked up her horn spoon and tasted the dish carefully; Colum attacked his with gusto.

'You like it?' Blanche Smithler came forward. Not sure of their response, she nervously wiped her hands on the snow-white apron wrapped round her slender waist.

Kathryn looked up. 'It's delicious. Stewed rabbit?'

'Aye,' Blanche replied. 'Old Raston, one of our grooms, there's not a rabbit alive he can't catch. I roast it until it is brown, cut it up and cook it further, mixing onions, red wine, ginger, pepper and salt with a pinch of clove. It's a favourite dish of the house, especially in winter.'

She moved away. Kathryn ate, trying to commit the recipe to memory. Afterwards a scullion gave them all a cup of hippocras, red wine sweetened with cinammon, ginger and a dash of sugar. Colum smacked his lips and leaned back against the high bench.

'Now,' he murmured, 'the questioning begins about theft, murder and treason.'

Chapter 3

Colum called the guests over and they sat in a semicircle round the hearth, sipping the hippocras Blanche Smithler served. The landlord claimed he had better things to do but Colum glowered at him and told him he would answer his questions either here or in the guildhall gaol. Luberon sat in the middle of the semicircle, his face full of self-importance, pleased that Kathryn and the Irishman had taken him into their confidence. Kathryn sat on the edge of the circle whilst Colum stood facing the guests, his back to the fire.

'Before any of you ask,' Colum began, 'I am the King's Commissioner in Canterbury. Master Simon Luberon here will attest to that. Mistress Swinbrooke is the city physician. It is her responsibility to view the corpse and assist me in any investigation or enquiry I choose to make. We are dealing with treason.'

Sir Gervase's jaw fell. 'What proof,' he stuttered. The old knight sprang to his feet. 'What proof do you have of that?'

'Sit down, sir!' Colum snapped. 'The unlawful slaying of an official and the theft of the King's taxes constitute treason. Sir Reginald Erpingham was definitely killed by a strong infusion of the poison belladonna. Now, today is Friday, the twentieth of December, the feast of St. Adelaide. The snow started falling when?'

'On Monday evening,' Father Ealdred offered.

'And Sir Reginald arrived?'

'That night,' the priest replied. 'We could judge by the skies that the snow was coming.'

'And when did you all arrive?'

A babble of voices answered his questions. Colum held his hand up. 'I shall deal with that later. However, you were all here by Wednesday evening?'

The guests agreed.

'And nothing untoward happened?'

'I told you,' Sir Gervase trumpeted. 'Sir Reginald woke up in a fright on Wednesday evening. The fellow was in a cold sweat, shivering like a maid.'

'Ah yes.' Colum moved away from the heat of the fire and sat on a stone plinth on the edge of the hearth. 'Tell me, Sir Gervase, exactly what happened?'

'Oh, it must have been well after midnight. I am a light sleeper.' The old knight glared around, his blue eyes protuberant, his white whiskers bristling. 'Comes from years of campaigning you know, sword by the bed. Old habits die hard.'

Kathryn hid her smile. Lady Margaret was not so successful and quietly giggled.

'Anyway,' Sir Gervase continued, 'ups I get. Reginald was screaming like a maid. I go out in the gallery and Erpingham is there in his nightgown, shaking like a leaf. I took him into my room, sat him down and gave him a good strong bowl of claret from my own jug.' Sir Gervase brushed his whiskers. 'The fellow said he had seen a vision, a woman dressed all in white, her face green-tinged, her eyes black and red like glowing coals, or so he said. She was standing at the foot of his bed staring at him.'

Kathryn watched the old man curiously then glanced along the line of guests. She felt uneasy. Everyone sat so calm and self-assured; they seemed unable to appreciate that any one of them could be guilty of treason and so suffer a dreadful death. Now this old knight was recounting an experience as if he really believed it. But how could Erpingham see a ghost?

'Sir Gervase.' Kathryn got up to stretch her tired muscles. 'Sir Gervase, I am sorry to interrupt, but you are sure of that?'

35

'Of course I am,' he replied. 'I am not a bloody liar. I am a Knight of the Shires. I've served on royal commissions myself. I was with Talbot in France, can't stand the goddamned frogs, jackanapes every one of them. I have seen sights, Mistress Swinbrooke, which would curdle your blood. Anyway'—he pointed at Standon, who sat toying with the buckle of his sword belt—'ask him, he joined us.'

Kathryn looked at the serjeant.

'It's the truth,' the soldier replied. 'I was sleeping at the foot of the stairs. I heard the scream and the doors opening.' He shrugged. 'You always can hear them, they creak so badly. Anyway, I go upstairs, Erpingham is with Sir Gervase. He's covered in sweat, white-faced, breathing fit to burst. You'd think he'd been swimming.'

'I heard it as well,' Smithler said. 'Our room is at the end of that gallery.' He glanced at the de Murvilles. 'You too?'

Husband and wife agreed. Kathryn smiled at the old knight.

'Sir Gervase, please continue.'

'Anyway, I calmed Erpingham down and he drank the claret. I told him it was a trick of the light.' He smirked at Smithler. 'Or something in the gravy the night before. I gave him a napkin to dry himself and took him back into his chamber.'

'I also went,' Standon added.

'And?' Colum asked.

'There was nothing except a foul smell: his night jar was full, you know, as if he had vomited or had the flux.'

'And this is what your servants found the next morning?' Kathryn asked the landlord.

'Yes, after our guests came down to break their fast, the scullions emptied the night jars. One of them said the room smelt like a cesspit.'

Kathryn nodded and stared into the fire.

'Mistress Swinbrooke,' Colum asked, 'what do you think?'

'I am a physician,' she replied. 'I deal with diseases and their ailments, the imbalance of humours in the body. However, I agree with Sir Gervase, something might have frightened Erpingham that night, terrified him out of his wits, to lose control over his bowels, bladder and stomach.' She looked at the mousy little clerk. 'Master Vavasour, on the night he saw his vision, had your master been drinking heavily?'

'Oh, no,' the little man squeaked, looking even more like a frightened rabbit, his nose twitching, his buck teeth protuberant. Kathryn was sure that, if they could, his ears would have started twitching as well.

'Oh, no,' Vavasour repeated. 'Master Erpingham liked his wine but he was fairly abstemious, two or three cups at the very most. That's correct, isn't it, Standon?'

'Aye,' the serjeant agreed. 'And he only ate what we did. Roast goose, tender and well cooked, covered in a parsley sauce.'

'And the next day?' Kathryn asked. 'The day he died?'

'Well, in the morning he seemed a bit ashamed.' Sir Gervase apparently regarded himself as the guests' self-appointed leader. 'He was a little trembly; he broke his fast on some bread and watered wine but, by noon, he was the same as ever.'

'Which was?' Kathryn persisted.

The old knight seemed to lose some of his confidence.

'Well?' she asked.

'I can answer that, Mistress Swinbrooke,' Father Ealdred offered. 'In the full light of day, Sir Reginald Erpingham is not a man you would seek out. After all, he was a tax collector.'

His reply provoked soft laughter from the group.

'So was St. Matthew,' Kathryn replied. 'What kind of man was Sir Reginald?'

'He was a cruel, heartless bastard,' Blanche Smithler said, her face white and drawn. She had lost some of her prettiness and shrugged off the warning tap on her arm by her husband. 'He often came here. He used to boast about how he could squeeze a penny out of an old crone or terrify some peasant. He was always feeling the bums of the maids or grabbing at their breasts. Aye, he was abstemious in drink but he liked his food and he was none too clean in his personal habits. He used to boast about his great house in Maidstone and how he was looking forward to being awarded some manor on the outskirts of Dover.'

Kathryn looked at Vavasour. 'Of course, you'd disagree with that, sir?'

The clerk opened his mouth to reply then looked away, nose twitching vigorously.

'The good wife speaks the truth,' Standon confirmed. He stared at Colum. 'Like you, Irishman, I am a professional soldier.' He smiled sourly. 'Though in the recent wars I fought for Lancaster. I was with the Bastard of Falconbridge when he tried to seize the Tower.'

Colum nodded sympathetically.

'Well, you know what happened to that?' Standon continued. 'Falconbridge lost his head. Like many others, I changed sides and sealed indentures with the Sheriff of Kent. I and the rest of my lads were Erpingham's guard; we have been since his Michaelmas tour around the shire.'

'And?' Colum asked.

'I've fought in battles,' Standon said. 'I've put flames to thatches, done my fair share of killing, God save me!' Standon blinked, his face losing some of its hardness. 'I wasn't always like that. In my youth I wanted to be a knight.' He blinked furiously. 'But, there again, you become what you are, not what you want to be.'

The taproom fell silent as this hard-bitten soldier opened his soul. Standon paused and rubbed his face with his hand.

'Erpingham was a bastard. He had a stone for a heart.'

'Did he have any family?' Kathryn asked.

'A wife,' Vavasour squeaked. 'He once had a wife but the poor woman died giving birth. He liked dogs,' the clerk added as if that was the only thing he could say in favour of his dead master.

'Was he honest?' Colum asked.

Vavasour looked so frightened Colum thought he was going to jump up and run away.

'Well?' the Irishman demanded.

'You know how it is,' Vavasour said timidly.

'Aye,' Colum replied. 'Show me an honest tax collector and I'll show you an Irishman who can fly.'

'By his own rights he was honest,' Standon added. 'Everyone has the right to appeal to the Sheriff or the King.'

'Oh yes?' Colum just grinned.

'Listen.' Kathryn pulled a chair forward. 'Master Smithler, this ghost, this haunted chamber? Erpingham always used it?'

'Aye, I have told you that.'

'And the painting, faded on the wall? It shows a devil, a young man and a woman.'

'Oh, there are many stories,' Blanche Smithler interrupted. 'They are all confused but, apparently, a young woman was murdered there or disappeared from the room.'

'And is it haunted?' Kathryn asked.

'People who have stayed there,' Smithler replied, 'talk of a feeling of unease, of sounds at night.' He shrugged. 'But we all have fanciful dreams.'

Luberon spoke up. 'If this tavern is as old as you say and a crime was committed here, there should be some record of it in the court rolls at the guildhall. Master Murtagh, I'll search those for you.'

'Has it ever been exorcised?' Father Ealdred asked. 'Blessed with holy water and salt?'

'It's too late for that now,' Sir Gervase muttered.

'And there are no secret entrances or passageways?' Kathryn asked. She ignored the old knight and stared at the landlord.

'I've already answered that,' he snapped. 'Search for yourself.'

'Oh, we may well do that,' Colum replied. 'And, sir, I must ask you to keep a civil tongue in your head.'

The landlord glanced away and hawked over his shoulder.

'And in the days before Erpingham died?' Colum continued, trying to ignore a cat which came padding across to claw amongst the rushes for a sliver of fat.

'Well, because of the snow,' Sir Gervase said, 'we were locked in here eating and drinking. The landlord has made a fine profit.'

'Aye, and I have served you well.'

'Never mind that,' Colum continued. 'You slept late, you ate, you drank . . .'

'Master Murtagh.' Lady Margaret straightened in her chair, daintily adjusting the veil over her lustrous hair. She stared coolly at him, her pretty mouth open; she glanced sideways at Kathryn and grinned as if she enjoyed flirting with this rough, dark-faced Irishman.

'My lady, I am waiting,' Colum said.

'I simply want to say,' she cooed rather quickly, 'that we played games like blind man's buff or told stories or diced. Those who could read, did so; books, Master Murtagh, if you know what they are?'

'Or perhaps write?' Kathryn interrupted. 'With quills, if you know what they are.'

Lady Margaret flounced back in her chair and stared petulantly at her husband.

'We were bored,' Lord Alan declared. 'We prayed for the snow to stop so we could continue our journey.'

'What happened the night Erpingham died?' Colum asked.

The old knight banged his sword on the floor and glowered round the group. 'I can answer that. We all dined here: haunch of venison, cooked in a thick sauce with vegetables roasted in its juice. Then the landlord opened his best claret, a small tun.' He gestured away towards the rafters. 'We sat here feasting.'

'And what time did Sir Reginald leave?'

'Sometime between the seventh and eighth hour,' Vavasour said. 'He said he was tired. He took his wine cup and went up to his chamber.'

'And where was everyone else?' Kathryn asked.

'Oh, we all stayed down here. Master Smithler was our host. His good wife supervised the cooks and scullions in the kitchen.'

'And no one visited Sir Reginald?'

A chorus of 'No's' greeted Kathryn's question.

'So.' Kathryn got to her feet. The heat from the fire was now strong and Colum's eyes were beginning to droop. 'Sir Reginald picks up his cup.' Kathryn picked up the goblet she'd brought down from Erpingham's chamber. 'In fact, this one. He goes upstairs to his bedchamber where he locks and bolts the door. He drinks the wine. Next morning he is found dead, poisoned whilst the taxes he has collected are stolen.' Kathryn rolled the cup between her hands. 'There can be a number of conclusions. So please help us with them.' She gently tapped Colum on the shoulder, fearful lest he fall asleep. 'First, Sir Reginald could have been poisoned at table.'

'Impossible!' Standon replied. 'I was sitting next to him. We shared the same trencher.'

Kathryn sighed. 'What about the wine?'

'Because of the inclement weather and my guests were paying so well,' Smithler replied, 'I opened a small tun, the best claret from Gascony. I gave each person at least one cup.'

'And Erpingham?' Kathryn asked.

'Well, he said he was tired; he took his goblet upstairs.'

'Could it have been poisoned before he left the table?' Colum asked, stirring himself.

'I doubt it,' Vavasour said.

'Why is that, Master clerk?' Kathryn asked.

The little man wriggled his nose and scratched the end of it thoughtfully. 'Well, the landlord gave us each a cup. I am not too fond of claret: Sir Reginald offered me a sip from his as a taster.'

'Was he that kindly?' Kathryn asked.

'No, no.' Vavasour shook his head. 'He drank from mine as well. What I am trying to say is that Erpingham's cup, mine and Master Standon's all became confused.' He struck his breast, eyes wide. 'God be my witness,' he said. 'I never tainted Sir Reginald's cup but, to the best of my knowledge, nor did anyone else. Indeed,' his voice rose even higher, 'with the cups being passed back and forth, people stretching and yawning after a good meal, it would have been impossible for any murderer to know which cup to poison.'

'So.' Kathryn moved away from the fire in the direction of the stairs, still clutching Erpingham's cup. 'Sir Reginald bade you good night?'

Vavasour agreed.

'And he goes upstairs?'

Again the nod of assent. Kathryn smiled at the old knight.

'Sir Gervase, perhaps you and Master Luberon could accompany me?'

And, with the old knight going before them, Kathryn and Luberon climbed the steep stairs into the gallery. They stopped outside Sir Gervase's chamber.

'Please.' Kathryn smiled. 'Let me see how these doors creak and groan.'

Sir Gervase happily obliged. He took the key from his wallet, unlocked the chamber door and pushed it slightly open.

'That's quiet enough,' Kathryn murmured.

Sir Gervase grinned mischievously. 'Ah, but listen to this.'

He pushed the door farther back on its hinges and Kathryn started at the strident screech of leather against iron. The old knight then closed it again, creating the same din. Kathryn's shoulders sagged.

'Lord above! I take your point, Sir Gervase. Such a noise would awaken the dead.'

They returned downstairs where the Irishman was waiting for her.

'You heard that, Colum?'

He scratched his head and grinned. 'Like a banshee's cry.'

Kathryn rejoined the watchful group.

'So,' she said again, putting the cup back on the mantel of the hearth. 'We have a group of people staying at the Wicker Man tavern. Two nights previous, the tax collector, Sir Reginald Erpingham, suffers a nightmare so dreadful he arouses Sir Gervase in the adjoining chamber. Last night all the guests attend a special dinner, deliciously cooked by Mistress Blanche. At the end of the meal, the landlord opens a small tun of claret.' Kathryn paused. 'According to what you all say, Sir Reginald then took his cup and retired to his chamber for the night. Now . . .' Kathryn rubbed a finger along her lips. 'As a physician, I would go on oath that Erpingham was deliberately and maliciously poisoned by an infusion of belladonna. We have also established, unless two or three people here are arrant liars, that Sir Reginald's food was not tainted, nor was the wine which he took to his chamber. Ergo,' she smiled at Luberon, 'as the scholars would say, someone must have visited Sir Reginald later that night and poisoned him. He or she then removed any trace of poison as well as the money from the saddlebags, replacing it with rocks.' Kathryn flailed her hands against her sides. 'Yet we know that such a person did not enter or leave by the window, nor is there any secret passageway, whilst Erpingham's door was locked and bolted from the inside.'

'I can guarantee that,' Standon said. 'When I broke the door down, the key was still in the lock, the bolts were pulled across and there wasn't any sign of violence in the room.' He stared at Vavasour for confirmation.

Sir Gervase spoke up, thoroughly enjoying Kathryn's bemusement. 'No one went into that room last night. I was in my chamber till well after midnight. I heard no sound outside nor did Erpingham's door creak.' The old man twirled his moustache. 'In fact, I heard no sound at all. Silent as the grave.' He chuckled sourly. 'There again, I now understand why.'

'Are you sure of that?' Colum asked.

'As God made little apples,' the old knight trumpeted.

'I can vouch for the same,' Standon said. 'Admittedly, I was at the foot of the stairs but I heard no commotion or fracas.'

'This is impossible.' Colum got to his feet, his face grey with exhaustion. 'How could a man in a locked, barred room be poisoned, have his gold taken, yet there's no sign of forced entry or how the murderer left?'

Kathryn stared round the close-set faces of the guests. She studied their faces for any glimmer of guilt; they gazed back expectantly as if this was some sort of game or troubadour's puzzle.

'Mistress Swinbrooke,' Luberon said, eager to help. 'Could the poison have been administered some other way? A tainted napkin or poison on the sheets?'

Kathryn shook her head. 'No, I examined the chamber carefully.'

She turned and stared into the flames of the fire, keeping her back to the rest of the tavern's guests to hide the hopelessness in her face. She glanced across at Colum who seemed equally dispirited and her heart lurched with compassion. It would be tempting, she reflected, to leave this, claim it was a mystery and go back to Ottemelle Lane. However, after Christmas, the King's pursuivants would arrive or, even worse, the royal Justices. They would ask what Colum had done and why the King's taxes had been so easily stolen?

'Is it possible,' Luberon wondered, 'that the poison was in some food or wine left in Sir Reginald's chamber?'

'I don't think so,' Vavasour said. 'First, when we entered there this morning, we found no trace of food or drink, apart from the goblet and that was untainted.'

'Tell me,' Father Ealdred asked. 'How do we know Sir Reginald didn't eat something before he came to dinner?'

'How long did the supper take?' Kathryn asked.

'About an hour and a half,' Father Ealdred replied.

'Belladonna acts quickly,' Kathryn declared. 'Really no more than twenty minutes.'

'And I was with Sir Reginald.' Vavasour sprang to his feet as if suddenly remembering something, one bony finger pointed to the rafters. 'I was with Sir Reginald in his chamber before dinner. We checked on the taxes and the saddlebags were full. I did not see Sir Reginald eat or drink anything.'

'And everyone attended the banquet?' Colum asked.

'Oh yes,' Sir Gervase replied. 'No one left except the landlord and his wife, who rose now and again to supervise the scullions and servants in the kitchen.'

Kathryn glanced across at the landlord. 'Master Smithler, we have taken up your time and that of your guests for far too long. However, Master Murtagh and I need to question each person separately. Is it possible'—she pointed to the window seat where the guests had first sat—'for us to sit over there?'

Smithler shrugged. 'If it's necessary and the King's business, then it has to be done.'

Kathryn smiled around at the rest of the group. 'I am sorry to trespass even further on your time but the weather is inclement and no one is travelling far.'

'Nor will anyone else,' Colum said firmly. 'As of this day, no one in this tavern has permission to leave Canterbury under pain of arrest.' He raised one hand to quell the hubbub. 'You are now the King's guests whether you like it or not. The usual claims can be presented to the Exchequer: money honestly spent will be honestly refunded.' He stared out through the window. 'Which is no great loss, as my good physician has declared; the weather is inclement and the roads are frozen.' He tapped the hilt of his sword warningly. 'On no account must anyone leave.'

Colum looked so threatening, his voice dark and sombre, no one dared to protest. Blanche Smithler filled their cups with hippocras. Kathryn and Colum went across and sat in the window seat, grateful to be away from the roaring heat of the fire.

'Colum, you look exhausted,' Kathryn murmured.

'I feel I could sleep for a month and a day,' the Irishman sighed. He sipped from the steaming cup. 'And this is the devil's own puzzle.'

Kathryn stared across where the guests were now clustered together, talking softly amongst themselves.

'One of them is a murderer,' she whispered. 'One, two or possibly all of them.' She closed her eyes and recalled the grey, red-blotched corpse lying stark beneath the sheets in that dreadful chamber. 'If I wasn't so tired . . .' she began.

'You'd what?' Colum teased.

'I don't know.' Kathryn breathed a sigh. 'I feel uneasy, Irishman.' She smoothed the front of her dress. 'It's hard to grasp. It's like that game when you try to pluck something slippery from a tub of water. Your eyes are blindfolded and you splash around but never grasp it.'

Kathryn stared through the mullioned window at the carpet of snow which stretched through the tavern gate and across the trackway to the open fields.

'There's some bond,' Kathryn continued, keeping her face away from the taproom. 'Some sort of conspiracy among the guests. Don't you find it strange, Colum, how they all seem to know Erpingham? Yet not one of them, even though he has been foully murdered, has a good word to say for him.'

Colum touched her knee gently. 'Kathryn, don't you think we should bring Luberon into this? He's looking as if he has lost a pound and found a shilling.'

Kathryn turned and smilingly beckoned the little clerk over. Luberon was sitting in a chair away from the guests, staring reproachfully across at them, and the way he waddled over to them so quickly and so cheerfully reminded Kathryn of a puppy she'd once owned. He pulled a stool over and sat next to Kathryn, perched above him on the window seat.

'What do you think, most subtle of clerks?' Kathryn teased.

'You were summoned to the tavern this morning,' Colum said. 'You saw the chamber?'

'Aye,' Luberon replied. 'Standon was on guard outside. Mistress Swinbrooke, I assure you of this. I examined that room very carefully: nothing had been tampered with when I returned with you.'

'I accept that,' Kathryn replied. 'I also know the claret left in Erpingham's cup had been there for some time: dust from the room had mingled with it.'

'What about the ghost?' Colum asked.

'A phantasm,' Kathryn replied. 'Sir Reginald was no angel and, even though he had a stone for a heart, ghosts lurk in everybody's soul. Perhaps it was a feeling of guilt or some nightmare from his past. Master Luberon'—she glanced at the clerk—'all the guests seem to know, as well as hate, Erpingham.'

'Well, he was a tax collector,' Luberon observed. 'Show me a popular tax collector, Mistress Swinbrooke, and I'll replace the stolen money myself. Don't forget, they are all Kentish-born, as was Erpingham. He'd be well known to them.'

'Ah, well,' Colum said. 'Let us begin.'

'Wait!' Kathryn warned. 'Are we sure about that chamber? Simon here has just said that all our guests are Kentish-born and they regularly come here.' She started as a rat suddenly appeared from under the boards beneath the window seat and scurried across the rushes, before disappearing into the gloomy corner next to the hearth.

'I intend to leave no stone unturned,' Colum said. 'I'll scour that chamber from ceiling to floor. If there's a secret passageway I'll discover it.'

'The ghost?' Luberon intervened. 'Could it have been man-made? Perhaps an attempt to frighten Erpingham to death?'

'For the moment,' Kathryn answered, 'let's deal with the living.' She raised her voice. 'Sir Gervase, if you would be so kind as to join us.'

The old knight, his ridiculous sword in its battered scabbard held before him, marched purposefully across, snapping his fingers at Smithler to fetch a chair. The landlord brought one over, slammed it down and stamped off. The old knight lowered himself gently into it, still grasping his sword by the cross hilt as if it were some staff of office.

'Sir Gervase,' Kathryn began, kicking Colum gently on his ankle to keep him awake. 'Why are you here at the Wicker Man? You hold lands . . . ?'

'Near Islip,' Sir Gervase bellowed. 'A moated manor house with barns, granges, plough and pasture lands.'

'So, why come to Canterbury?' Kathryn asked.

'To pray before the Blessed Martyr's bones!' Sir Gervase trumpeted. He leaned forward, lowering his voice. 'I am one of them, you know.'

'One of what?' Colum asked.

'One of the murderers,' Sir Gervase whispered conspiratorially.

'You mean Erpingham?'

'Don't be stupid, man!' Sir Gervase tapped his sword on the floor. 'I am a descendant of one of those knights who murdered Becket. My mother was a de Broc, you know, Becket's most ardent enemy. So, every year, around Christmas, the time of Blessed Thomas's death, I make my own small pilgrimage. I stay at the Wicker Man; Smithler doesn't like me and I don't like him but it's a good tavern. The beds are clean, the fleas are banished and the rats know their place. Not like in France. Lord, Mistress, I could tell you tales—'

'Yes, yes,' Kathryn tactfully interrupted. 'And you knew Sir Reginald?'

The old knight's genial face became hard, lips curling in a snarl. 'Knew him? Yes, I knew him!' he hissed. 'And I'm glad, do you know that, Mistress? I am glad the wicked bastard is dead!'

Chapter 4

*S*urprised at the venom in the old man's voice, Colum asked, 'Are you saying that you wanted Erpingham dead?'

'Don't put words in my mouth, Irishman,' Sir Gervase snarled, banging his sword on the floor. 'All I am saying is that I am glad he received his just deserts, both in this life and the next.'

'Why?' Colum asked.

'He was as hard as flint, cold as ice. He neither feared God nor man. Above all, he was a thief.'

'What proof do you have of this?' Kathryn asked.

Sir Gervase's eyes slid away. 'Gossip, whispering in the corners.'

Kathryn touched the old man gently on his hand.

'You are wise,' she flattered him. 'And shrewd, Sir Gervase. There's more, isn't there?'

Mollified and flattered by Kathryn's concern, the old man smiled.

'He was a lecher. God help the poor widow who couldn't pay some impost or tariff. Erpingham would ask her to pay it in kind. He seemed to enjoy baiting and blackmailing some pretty, defenceless woman.'

'And then he'd pay the levy for her?' Kathryn asked.

'Show me a poor tax collector,' Sir Gervase replied.

'Why didn't you confront him with this?' she asked.

'Erpingham was a lawyer, he trained at the Inns of Court. You've heard the story, Mistress Swinbrooke?'

Kathryn shook her head.

'Once the devil saw a lawyer kill a viper outside a stable; the devil grinned because it reminded him of Cain killing Abel.'

'You don't like lawyers?' Colum asked.

'Aye, I don't like lawyers but I hated Erpingham. If I'd had the proof I'd have complained direct to the King's chamber at Westminster.'

'Yes, yet you comforted him when he suffered the nightmare?'

'Oh, I gave him a cup of claret,' Percy replied. He leaned closer, his face now ugly with hate. 'But I did enjoy seeing him suffer.'

'And his death?' Colum persisted.

Sir Gervase held his sword up by the cross hilt.

'I swear by all that is holy, I wished him dead but his blood is not on my hands!'

Kathryn heard a movement across the taproom: she glimpsed Vavasour slipping up the stairs and realized abruptly what was missing.

'Master Vavasour,' she called. 'Please don't go upstairs!'

The little clerk shuffled back down, his face crestfallen, shoulders sagging. Colum caught the warning in Kathryn's voice. He stood up and walked over to the group of travellers.

'You are to stay down here!' he ordered. He looked over his shoulder. 'Master Luberon, of your kindness, please guard the chamber.'

Colum walked back towards the window seat.

'Are you finished with me?' the old knight asked; he smiled apologetically at Kathryn. 'Mistress Swinbrooke, excuse my bad manners, my lack of charity and heartlessness, but I couldn't abide the sight of that tax collector!'

'Did you have dealings with him?' Kathryn asked.

Sir Gervase's head went back. 'Good Lord, woman, no! My bailiffs and stewards dealt with the likes of Erpingham though they informed me about the gossip from the villages.'

'And the night Erpingham died?'

'Mistress, I have told you all that I know. No one went near Erpingham's chamber.'

Kathryn thanked him and beckoned Vavasour and Standon across as the old knight, apparently relieved, slipped away to join the rest.

The clerk sat down on the stool Luberon had vacated, Standon next to him.

'Where were you going, Master Vavasour?' Kathryn asked sweetly.

The little man tried to clean a food stain from his threadbare hose.

'Mistress Swinbrooke asked you a question,' Colum insisted.

'I asked,' Kathryn continued, watching Vavasour squirm in embarrassment, 'because there is something missing, isn't there?' She leaned closer. Vavasour glanced up, licking his thin lips as he tried to control his panic. At first he had been terrified of the dark-visaged Irishman with his hooded eyes, swarthy face and tousled hair. Vavasour had moved amongst soldiers too often not to recognise a professional killer, but this woman physician frightened him even more. She, with her clear grey eyes, smooth skin and sweet face, was as sharp as a razor.

'I know why you were going up there,' Kathryn said. 'And I shall tell you, Master Vavasour. Here is Sir Reginald Erpingham, a knight of the shire, a lawyer, a tax collector, a man of wealth and substance. However, apart from his clothes and the saddlebags which contained the King's silver, where are the rest of his possessions? Surely he would travel in more comfort and luxury? Where is the pomander he'd hold against his nose when he had to talk to some sweat-soaked steward or mud-covered bailiff? Where's his change of clothes, boots, personal monies and documents? All we've seen are the clothes Erpingham wore the evening he died!' She squeezed Colum's wrist. 'Master Murtagh, if you would be so kind, go up to the chamber and bring down the dead man's clothes, particularly his belt and wallet.'

Colum obeyed. Kathryn stared out of the window, humming a tune. For the first time since she had come to this dreadful inn, she felt a small glow of pleasure: the same elation as when she treated a patient and discovered the cause of some mysterious ailment. Colum came thundering back down the stairs; across one shoulder were the saddlebags, Erpingham's clothes slung over the other.

'Master Luberon sends you his compliments.' He grinned at Kathryn. 'And asks you not to be too long. I have asked him to search for any hidden door or secret passageway.'

Colum put the clothes down in front of Kathryn. She picked up the fine linen shirt, the pure leather jerkin with its wool lining, a pair of quilted riding gloves and thick woollen hose. Thrust down one long riding boot, Kathryn found Sir Reginald's belt, wallet and, in the other boot, a long Welsh stabbing knife in a decorated scabbard. Kathryn scrutinised the lining of the belt, undid the buckle strap on the wallet and drew out a number of coins and three large keys tied together with twine. She held these up.

'Well, well,' she murmured. 'Are you going to tell me, Master Vavasour, why these are so important that you were stealing back to your dead master's chamber to collect them?'

Vavasour was now quivering with fright; even his wispy hair seemed to be standing up in terror. He opened and closed his mouth, swallowed and blinked so furiously that, had it been any other occasion, Kathryn would have burst out laughing.

'I know nothing of this,' Standon growled, shuffling his boots.

'No, but Master Vavasour does,' Kathryn declared. 'Oh, for God's sake, man, don't be so frightened! You were going to steal these keys. Why? Or shall I tell you? Sir Reginald, I suspect, rented a house here in Canterbury. When he visited the city he would sometimes stay there, wouldn't he? Keeping a change of clothing, valuable items and God knows what else? Am I right, Master clerk?'

Vavasour nodded.

'Which brings up another question,' Kathryn continued. 'Or rather two. First, if Sir Reginald had a house in Canterbury, why come and stay here? Secondly, what, Master Vavasour, were you going to do with these keys?'

'You are speaking the truth,' Standon muttered. 'We arrived in Canterbury on Monday. I and my escort were told to stay here; Sir Reginald and Vavasour left for a while and then came back.' He snapped his fingers. 'Of course, Erpingham's personal saddlebag is missing.'

'Well, well, well.' Colum smiled at Vavasour. 'What do we have here? Were those tax panniers filled with rocks before Sir Reginald ever arrived at the Wicker Man?' He leaned across and patted the little man on the shoulder. 'What game is being played here?' he demanded.

'Master Murtagh.' Standon held his hands up placatingly.

Kathryn stared pityingly at Vavasour who now looked as if he was on the verge of swooning through sheer terror.

'Master Murtagh,' Standon repeated. 'I cannot vouch for what Sir Reginald or Vavasour did, but when we first arrived here, the panniers containing the taxes were left with me.'

'How do you know the silver was there?'

'I asked Sir Reginald to open them before he left,' Standon repllied.

The hard-faced serjeant coughed to clear his throat. 'I'm no fool, Irishman. I do not want to end my life on a scaffold, either for robbing the King's taxes or even on the suspicion that I did.'

'Master Vavasour,' Kathryn insisted. 'So far you have committed no crime. If you tell the truth, you have nothing to fear.'

The clerk stared at her and, in spite of his fear, Kathryn glimpsed a calculating look in the little man's eyes. You are not as frightened as you pretend, she concluded; you are one of those who appear to dither, but underneath you are quite cold.

'Sir Reginald does have a house,' Vavasour explained. 'A small, well-secured and costly furnished tenement in St. Alphage's Lane.'

'What does he use it for?' Kathryn asked.

'As you said, Mistress, Sir Reginald did not really trust taverns or tavern-keepers. Sometimes he would reside there or use it to store valuable property.'

'So, why did he come here?' Colum asked.

Vavasour shrugged, his thin shoulders wriggling. 'I asked him the same question. Erpingham declared that he enjoyed the food, the hospitality and other people's company.'

You are lying, Kathryn thought. 'Listen.' She stretched her back to ease the cramps. 'We have heard little good about your dead master, God rest him.'

'Sir Reginald was thorough,' Vavasour replied. 'He was a skilled and ruthless searcher-out of the King's prerogative. He cannot be faulted for that. He made his enemies but—'

'But few friends,' Kathryn finished.

'He made no friends,' Standon interrupted. 'He was cold and hard in demanding what was the King's.'

'And the night he died?' Kathryn insisted. 'What you've told us is the truth?'

'Erpingham ate and drank with us,' the serjeant said, 'then retired for the night. I saw no one else go up to his room. I owe nothing to Master Vavasour here but I can vouch that he spoke the truth: there was confusion over the wine cups and I saw no interference with them.'

'Tell me,' Colum interjected. 'Did your master usually suffer from nightmares?'

'He slept like a child,' Vavasour replied.

'So, what disturbed his sleep that night?' Kathryn said.

'If I knew that, Mistress, I'd tell you as I would anything else.'

Kathryn thanked and dismissed them. The de Murvilles came next. They sat, clasping each other's hands. Lord Alan was likeable: fresh-faced, he gazed candidly at her whilst he spoke softly with a gentle hint of self-mockery. Lady Margaret was pleasant enough though rather spoilt: her pretty face was pulled in a frown of bored indifference to the proceedings.

'Must we really stay here?' she asked petulantly.

'Yes, you really must,' Colum mimicked back. He leaned over to add, before Lord Alan could take offence, 'Believe me,' Colum whispered, 'to kill a royal official is one thing. To murder a King's tax collector and steal the Crown's monies is another. My masters in London would have no qualms in seizing everyone involved and sending them to the Tower until a satisfactory conclusion is reached.'

'Why are you here?' Kathryn abruptly asked.

'We were returning from Dover,' Lord Alan replied. 'My wife's father is Constable of the castle there. We joined a small band of pilgrims and, because of the threatening weather, turned off into Canterbury.'

'And you have lodged here before?'

'On our journeys to Dover, yes.'

'And did you know Sir Reginald?'

'He was a tax collector in this county,' Lord Alan said. 'Regrettably, we fell under his jurisdiction.'

'And did you have dealings with him?'

'Where possible, not!' Lady Margaret snapped. 'He may have been a knight but he was base-born in his manners. He didn't know how to treat a lady.'

'Do you have personal experience of that?' Kathryn asked.

Lady Margaret blushed and glanced away.

'We hardly knew him,' Lord Alan declared. 'When we found him here, we kept our distance. Never once did I, or my wife, even bother to notice him.' He smiled wearily. 'Little difference that made: Erpingham seemed pleased by the discomfort he caused.'

'And of his death?'

The young man ran a finger round the collar of his tunic.

'At table we kept well away from him. Last night, he retired to bed. We followed sometime later. We heard nothing until Standon began pounding on the door early this morning.'

After the de Murvilles had left, seeking permission to return to their own chamber, Tobias and his wife came over. Mistress Smithler smiled pleasantly; her husband, however, remained as ungracious as ever.

'Will I be recompensed for all this?' he moaned.

'Any charges,' Colum repeated, 'must be sent to the Exchequer or to the guildhall.'

'Did you like Sir Reginald?' Kathryn asked.

'Yes, I did,' Tobias replied defiantly. 'He came here often. He was a good guest, he ate well, ordered numerous meals and demanded the best stabling for his horses. Of course, I bloody well liked him!' He threw off his wife's warning hand. 'Erpingham always settled his bills, except this one and who'll pay that, eh?'

'Why did he come here?' Kathryn persisted.

'We looked after him.'

'For any other reason?'

'If there was,' Tobias retorted, 'then he didn't tell us.'

'Did you know anything about him?'

'He was a tax collector,' Blanche Smithler said. 'He was not well liked but his purse was well lined. We had no real dealings with him: our taxes are collected by the city bailiffs.'

'Did he talk to anyone in particular?' Colum asked. 'Apart from Vavasour or Standon?'

'He had long discourse with Father Ealdred.'

'When was this?'

'Yesterday afternoon.'

'About anything in particular?' Kathryn asked.

'They were in a corner where no one could hear them.'

'And you never talked to him?' Colum asked.

'Very little,' Smithler said. 'We liked his money.'

'And when he had the nightmare?'

'We were disturbed,' Blanche remarked. 'But Sir Gervase seemed to have everything under control so we left it at that.'

'And at the supper before he died?'

'We joined our guests at table,' the landlord replied. 'We are good hosts. My wife was busy in the kitchen, running backwards and forwards; the cooks and scullions have to be supervised properly, otherwise sauces are spoilt and the meat is ill cooked. Oh,' the landlord cleared his throat, 'and before you ask, Sir Reginald always demanded that chamber. God knows why! I tell you this, Master Murtagh, my wife and I know nothing about his death. We are concerned with profit and nothing else.'

They got to their feet; Tobias strode away, his wife trailing behind him, smiling apologetically over his shoulder at Kathryn.

'Remembering my Chaucer,' Colum murmured, 'Master Tobias Smithler would make a good physician.'

Kathryn tapped him gently on the ankle. 'Irishman, you are still in my ill favour.' She smiled. 'You look tired.'

'Well.' Colum stretched. 'We'll see the priest and go; sufficient for the day is the evil thereof. Or, as Chaucer's squire says, "The nurse of good digestion is natural sleep." '

'I am sorry, Colum, we have still to go to Blunt's house.'

'Can't it wait?'

'I doubt it. Master Luberon was most insistent.'

Colum was about to protest when Father Ealdred came across and sat down. Kathryn studied the priest closely: smooth-faced, his tonsure was neatly cut, his eyes friendly but guarded.

' "And the last shall be first and the first shall be last," ' Ealdred began, quoting from the gospels.

'I am sorry we had to keep you, Father.' Kathryn caught his implied rebuke. 'But, in these matters, it is best to question each individual.'

The priest moved his hand, a delicate movement, as if absolving Kathryn's offence.

'Why are you in Canterbury? And why stay at the Wicker Man?' Colum asked abruptly.

'I am parish priest of St. Swithin's in Meopham,' Eldred began. 'A bustling, thriving parish. I thought I'd come and visit the shrine and buy supplies for my chancery: vellum, ink, new quills as well as provisions for Christmas.'

'You visit Canterbury often?'

'Once every quarter: I won't return until Passion Week, then again at midsummer.'

'When were you last here?'

'Just before Michaelmas.'

'And you always stay at the Wicker Man?' Colum said. 'Surely you have priestly friends in Canterbury who might give you comfortable lodgings?'

Ealdred laughed nervously. 'I prefer coming here.'

'You seem concerned, Father,' Kathryn observed. 'Did you know Sir Reginald?'

'He collected taxes in my parish.'

'But did you know him well? After all, some of the guests say you were in deep conversation with him.'

Ealdred looked angrily over his shoulder.

'Father.' Kathryn caught him gently by the sleeve. 'We can't sit and chat till the Second Coming: Erpingham's death is an urgent matter.'

The priest coughed and cleared his throat.

'I was trying to hear his confession,' he whispered. 'Sir Reginald was a truly evil man, Mistress Swinbrooke. He flattered neither flesh nor face. He no more feared God than he did man.'

'And yet you hardly knew him?' Kathryn asked.

'The truth is, Mistress, Erpingham was a hard man. The others have probably told you: no widow was safe with him. He was a lecher born and bred. I sat in my confessional and listened to the stories of my parishioners. When I met him here I pleaded with him to change. I warned him of God's judgement and the fires of hell.'

'And what was Erpingham's answer?'

'He just laughed.'

'Did he go to church?' Kathryn asked.

'If he did, I never knew about it. As a tax collector, he often stayed days in my parish, but never once did Sir Reginald darken the door of God's house.' Ealdred's voice dropped to a whisper. 'I believe he was a warlock.'

'A witch?' Colum asked.

'Witch, warlock, magus. There's a woman in my village; she came and confessed to a terrible sin. How Sir Reginald had abused her and, in his passion, declared he had no love for Christ or his Church but put his trust in the Dark Lords of the air.'

'Do you think that was true?' Kathryn asked. 'Why should a tax collector tell this to a woman he was seducing?'

'Isolda is a young widow,' Ealdred replied carefully. 'Erpingham came to her house and said, for favours granted, he would ignore the tax assessment upon her. She had two bairns; her husband had been killed in the recent wars and so she agreed. The following night she sent the children to a neighbour's house and Erpingham came back.' The priest paused, pushing his hands up the voluminous sleeves of his gown. 'You can guess the rest,' he murmured. 'But one thing Isolda remembers, she had a crucifix hanging in her bedchamber. Erpingham insisted that it be turned against the wall whilst he cast some light powder around the place, murmuring an incantation. Isolda asked him why and Erpingham made his reply.'

'Was Vavasour or Standon part of this?' Colum asked.

The priest shook his head. 'Standon is what he appears to be: a hard-faced soldier carrying out his tasks. Vavasour . . .' The priest trailed off and pulled a face. 'Erpingham's shadow. A little weasel. It is wrong to judge anyone living or dead but Erpingham and Vavasour both richly deserved each other. Sir Reginald, I think, used to boast about his conquests to his clerk.'

'Did you mention Isolda to Sir Reginald?' Kathryn asked.

'No, I kept myself to generalities. Sir Reginald was a vindictive man and that poor woman would have suffered.' The priest beamed with pleasure. 'Now I'll take good news back to her. God forgive me but I'm glad Erpingham is dead!'

'Do you believe in ghosts, Father?' Kathryn changed tack.

'I believe in what St. Paul says, Mistress Swinbrooke: the devil goes about like a roaring lion seeking whom he may devour. You are talking of Erpingham's nightmare? I say it was a judgement from God.'

'And you know nothing about his death?'

'No, Mistress, I do not.' Ealdred pushed his chair back. 'May I go now? I have yet to celebrate Mass.'

Kathryn wondered about the priest's relationship with Isolda but decided to keep a still tongue. Ealdred got to his feet and was about to go, then abruptly sat down again.

'Mistress Swinbrooke, surely you understand what I say? Especially you?'

'Why do you say that, Father?'

'I know about you, Mistress. You have a good reputation in the city. Father Cuthbert at the Poor Priests' Hospital speaks highly of you.'

Kathryn blushed at his compliment.

'You are a widow, are you not? You can feel for poor Isolda? Your husband,' the priest rushed on, 'Alexander Wyville, he left with the Lancastrians to fight at Barnet?'

Kathryn stared past the priest watching the cat in the inglenook carefully cleaning itself. Alexander Wyville, she thought, the wife beater, the drunken oaf. She glanced back at the priest.

'I am not a widow, truly, Father. As Father Cuthbert must have told you, I do not know whether my husband is alive or dead.'

'I am sorry,' Ealdred said.

'Why, Father? I am not.'

Ealdred caught the anger in Kathryn's eyes and swiftly excused himself.

'You have a clacking tongue, Mistress Swinbrooke,' Colum muttered. 'The poor fellow was only asking for sympathy.'

'Irishman,' Kathryn replied, 'he has my sympathy but my husband Alexander Wyville has not.'

Colum was distracted by this sudden turn of events. 'Surely news must soon come through of his whereabouts?'

Kathryn rose to her feet and turned to look out of the window.

'Colum, if I have told you once, I have told you a hundred times. I married Alexander Wyville and he turned out to be a drunken bully who deserted me to seek his fortune in the Lancastrian camp. If he is dead, then God have mercy on him! But if he is alive and returns, I shall ask the church courts for an annulment of our marriage.'

Colum sighed; any mention of Wyville always enraged Kathryn.

'Well.' He got to his feet. 'For the time being, we are finished here.'

They called for Luberon and as the clerk hurried downstairs, eager to be away from that lonely, sombre room, Colum summoned the guests.

'You are not to leave here until these matters are finished.'

'And the corpse?' Smithler asked.

'Have it sheeted and coffined,' Colum replied, 'and taken down to one of the city churches.'

'Holy Cross,' Luberon intervened. 'Such corpses are always buried there. If anyone later wishes to claim it, they will be free to do so.'

Colum and Kathryn wrapped their cloaks around themselves and followed Luberon into the tavern yard whilst Tobias Smithler brusquely slammed the door behind them.

'A pretty pottage,' Luberon murmured. He stared up at the sky: the clouds were now beginning to break and a weak sun was struggling through. 'But we should be grateful for small mercies: the snow has stopped.'

'A thaw has begun,' Colum cheerfully remarked. 'I told you, Kathryn, by nightfall Canterbury will be awash.'

Kathryn stared up at the window of the chamber where Erpingham's corpse lay.

'Aye,' she replied. 'But will we be any wiser about events here? What do you think, Irishman?'

' "What is a farthing worth when split twelve ways?" ' Colum replied, quoting from Chaucer.

'Oh, sweet Lord,' Kathryn breathed. 'None of your homely wisdom now.'

Colum gestured back towards the tavern. 'A man has been killed,' he continued softly. 'He goes up to his chamber with a goblet of wine. His door and window shutters are locked and bolted. No one visits him nor does he leave again. Yet the next morning he is murdered and the King's silver is gone.'

'I wonder where it is?' Luberon piped up. 'I mean the taxes?'

Colum gestured helplessly round the yard. 'You could hide every coin of the realm here.' He nodded back at the tavern. 'Either one or all of them are lying.'

'What I find suspicious,' Kathryn declared, 'is their deep hatred for Erpingham; it is no coincidence that some, or all of them, were in that tavern when he died.'

'Let's leave it for a while,' Colum suggested. 'Mistress Kathryn, I am freezing, starving and I need a few hours sleep.'

'We have to visit Blunt's house,' Luberon declared sharply.

Colum groaned: he felt dead on his feet. In the midmorning light his face seemed grey and dark circles ringed his eyes. Kathryn, too, had little enthusiasm for further questioning, for becoming involved in the sordid aspects of more macabre murders.

'Master Luberon,' she insisted. 'You must excuse us. Go to Erpingham's house in St. Alphage's Lane. Ensure the doors are sealed until we can all visit it.'

'And Blunt?' Luberon persisted. 'I have to make a report for the council.'

Kathryn grabbed his podgy hand and squeezed it affectionately.

'Simon, Simon, most of the council are hiding in their own houses, wrapped in rugs before roaring fires. Blunt has been taken, the matter will wait for a while.' She smiled. 'Otherwise both the King's Commissioner in Canterbury, not to mention his physician, will be ill with the ague.'

Luberon reluctantly agreed and dolefully accompanied them back into Castle Row and up into Westgate. He said he would see them later and stamped off towards the High Street, grumbling under his breath about public duty and the need to get things done immediately.

Kathryn watched him go. She stared longingly down Hill Lane, where the houses and shops were still shuttered and closed. Only a few children played in the streets, their cries ringing clear in the cold morning air.

'Well?' Colum asked. 'Is it a warm hearth and good food?'

'Colum, come with me for a while.'

The Irishman kicked at the dirt-stained snow.

'Kathryn, I'll either go home and sleep or I shall lie down here until some poor, good woman has mercy on me.'

Kathryn looked wistfully at the spire of St. Mildred's Church.

'I would like to visit there.' She pointed. 'My father lies buried in the transept before Our Lady's Chapel.'

'Kathryn, you can go some other time.'

'No, no.' She shook her head. 'I was there two days ago. I saw Richard Blunt and his son, painting in the sanctuary, breathtaking, colourful scenes. I just want to look at them again. I want to know why a man capable of portraying such beauty could leave God's house, walk through the streets of Canterbury and cold-bloodedly kill his wife and two young men.'

Colum chewed on his lip. He knew Kathryn's moods: she was

stubborn and single-minded. She would always do what she had set her heart upon yet he could feel his legs trembling from the cold. He grasped her hand, linking her arm through his and turned back in the direction of Ottemelle Lane.

'Listen,' he said. 'Fill my stomach with Thomasina's food. Let me sleep for a few hours and I'll go with you to Byzantium!'

'With an offer like that,' Kathryn grinned, 'how could any one refuse?'

Chapter 5

At the Wicker Man, Father Ealdred returned to his own room. He collected his small phial of holy oil and walked along to the dead man's chamber.

'What are you doing, Father?' Standon asked, lounging against the door lintel.

Ealdred stared into the shadow-filled room.

'It's so sombre,' he whispered. 'Tell me, Standon, do you believe a house or room can be haunted?'

Standon just shrugged.

'Well, I am going to bless Sir Reginald Erpingham,' Ealdred declared. 'He may have died unshriven but his soul may still be in limbo hovering between heaven and earth awaiting judgement.'

'If you ask me,' Standon growled, 'the bastard's long gone to sizzle in the flames of hell!'

Ignoring him, Ealdred entered the room and pulled back the bed drapes; he stared down at the sheet covering Erpingham's corpse and recalled the words of his bishop: 'We do not know what the soul does after death. The stopping of the heart and of the blood coursing in the veins does not mean that the soul has yet gone to its Maker.'

Ealdred pulled back the sheet and knelt beside the bed. He guiltily remembered his own secrets. He had not told the Irishman or Mistress Swinbrooke the whole truth, yet here he was preparing to give this evil man absolution. Ealdred swallowed hard and whispered the words of the ritual: 'At the hour of your death, in danger of eternal damnation, I, Ealdred, priest of the parish of St. Swithin's, do by the infinite merits of Christ's passion and death, absolve you from all your sins.'

Erpingham's bleak, sharp-nosed face lay gaping upwards. Ealdred stood up, undid the small phial he carried and, hiding his distaste, anointed the grey flesh of the dead tax collector: the brow, eyes, mouth, the ears, chest, feet and hands. The priest tried not to look at the red blotches now turning a deep scarlet.

'Too much was used!' Ealdred whispered. 'Too much was used!'

'What was that, Father?'

The priest whirled round. Vavasour had crept quietly near the bed. The little clerk now reminded Ealdred more of a hungry rat than a frightened rabbit: his eyes narrowed, his yellow buck teeth jutted out.

'I was just saying the prayers for the dead.'

Vavasour tapped the dead man on the ankle. 'Much good it will do him,' the clerk retorted. 'Gone the way of all flesh, has old Erpingham. And a very wicked boy indeed, eh, Standon?'

'You are pleased he is dead?' Ealdred asked.

'Pleased? I'm delighted, though it's a pity that surly Irishman and his sharp-eyed doxy seized those keys.'

'Did he have so much to hide?' Ealdred asked.

Vavasour walked round the bed, coming so close Ealdred could smell his fetid breath.

'Now, now, Father,' Vavasour whispered. 'We all have our little secrets, don't we? I wager you told them the story about Isolda: I also could tell them a few tales.' Vavasour smirked. 'I could tell them stories about you. Why you and the rest are here at the Wicker Man. Who knows?' The smirk faded from Vavasour's face, his lips curled in a sneer. 'I might even tell them who killed old Erpingham!'

'What do you mean?' Ealdred asked.

Vavasour stared down at his dirty fingernails. 'Sir Reginald told me how Isolda screamed and screamed, noisy, very noisy, she was.'

Ealdred grabbed the man by the front of his jerkin.

'Take your hands off me, Father!'

The priest pushed him away.

'It's not over yet,' Vavasour smirked.

'What isn't over?' Sir Gervase Percy, disturbed by the sounds, now stood in the doorway behind them. Vavasour smiled in mock innocence.

'Oh, nothing's over yet, is it? And don't you fool me, Sir Gervase, stumbling round like an old war horse, banging your sword on the ground. You hated my master.'

'Aye, everyone did,' Standon interrupted.

Vavasour, unabashed, walked towards the serjeant.

'Aye, even you, Standon. Did you tell the Irishman how Erpingham used to collect taxes from your mother?'

The soldier took a step forward, bumping into the unhinged door. Vavasour quickly stepped back, one finger pointing to the ceiling.

'Now, now, no violence. Because if I begin to chatter, no one here is safe.' He stalked out of the room, shouldering his way between Standon and Percy. 'And always remember,' he shouted, 'this is not yet finished for there's many a slip 'twixt cup and lip!'

Kathryn lay resting, staring up at the heavily embroidered tester of her four-poster bed. She and Colum had arrived home to find Thomasina had taken everything in hand. The house was clean and bright as a new pin, the kitchen sweet with a chicken roasting on the spits, and a creamy sauce of ground almonds, cloves, peppercorns, ginger, sugar, vinegar and egg yolks stood warming in the small oven next to the hearth. Everyone was delighted to see Colum: Wuf, jumping up and down with excitement, shouted.

'He's back again! He's back again! He's back again!'

Agnes stared, round-eyed, at this tall Irishman who could brave the wilds of Kent. Even Thomasina, her face red and sweaty from the fire, muttered something about a bad penny always turning up. Colum squeezed her waist, tickling her and not letting her go until Thomasina laughingly declared her relief at the Irishman's return. Colum refused anything to drink: he declared himself exhausted and, if Kathryn had not pushed him up the stairs, would have fallen asleep on his feet in the kitchen. Kathryn herself had rested for a while. She now propped herself up on one elbow and looked across at the hour candle. It must be about four in the afternoon and her patients, whom Thomasina had turned away earlier in the day, would be returning. She sighed and swung her legs off the bed, put on a pair of soft buskins and washed her hands and face in a bowl of rose water. She dried herself carefully with a soft woollen napkin, tied her hair neatly behind her head and went down to the kitchen.

Wuf immediately ran up, holding a wooden carving.

'I did it myself!' he shouted. 'Colum brought me the wood and Thomasina gave me the tools!'

Kathryn absent-mindedly agreed with everything he said, then looked at the carving and saw what the foundling had done. She took it carefully and sat at the foot of the stairs.

'Did you do this, Wuf?'

The little boy's pale face shone with pleasure, a mask of delight from the tip of his pointed chin to his untidy, blond hair.

'Oh, of course. When I was in the camp, the soldiers used to teach me.'

Kathryn stared down admiringly at the hunting scene the little boy had carved: a man on his horse, half turned in the saddle, blowing a horn; in front of him a greyhound raced towards a bush hiding a cheeky-faced fox. Kathryn glanced up.

'How old are you, Wuf?'

'I have been here about six months,' Wuf replied, ignoring the question. 'Does that make me your son?'

Kathryn hugged him close, kissing him on his dirt-stained cheek. 'You are whatever you want to be, Wuf: my son, my brother, my friend.'

'Can I be your husband?' Wuf's hand flew to his lips. 'Oh, I am sorry,' he gasped. 'You have two, haven't you?'

Kathryn threw her head back and laughed.

'I have one husband, Wuf. I have explained this to you before and, what I haven't, you've probably heard by hiding behind the kitchen door: Alexander Wyville went to the wars and he's not come back.'

'Oh yes, he's a bad bastard!'

'Wuf!'

'Well, that's what Thomasina told the Irishman. If Wyville comes back, will the Irishman kill him?'

'I'll kill you!' a voice declared from the top of the stairs. Colum stood there, his face heavy with sleep.

'No, you won't!' Wuf cried, dancing up and down. 'Thomasina will get you! Thomasina will get you!'

'Look what Wuf has done,' Kathryn exclaimed, trying to divert the conversation.

Colum came down the stairs and stared. 'It's a Misericord!' he said with surprise. 'You know, a carving on a seat of a church stall.' He squeezed between Kathryn and the wall and sat on the stairs. 'How old are you, Wuf?' He asked the same question Kathryn had.

'Oh, I was just going to say,' Wuf replied. 'One of the soldiers, he thought I'd just passed my eleventh summer. He was a carpenter. He taught me how to do this. 'He said you had to have a . . .'

'Good eye?' Kathryn queried.

'That's it. Anyway,' Wuf continued breathlessly, 'it's a present for you, Kathryn. Do you like it?'

Before she could even thank him, Wuf had danced away, shouting did Agnes want a present as well? Kathryn got to her feet, straightening the creases from the back of her dress.

'You smelt the food, Irishman?'

'If I don't eat soon,' he murmured, 'I'll eat Thomasina!'

'Quite a mouthful,' Kathryn replied. 'But first, I must see to my patients.'

Colum headed for the kitchen to see what he could beg, and Kathryn walked down into the large room at the front of the house which, God willing, she would soon turn into a shop. She stared round appreciatively. Colum had worked well: the counter was of new-grain wood: the shelves and small cupboards on the wall were straight and neatly polished. She had applied for her licence from the Spicers' Guild and, when the roads were passable, the extra supplies she had ordered from London would arrive. Kathryn felt her stomach tingle with excitement; she'd sell not only home-grown herbs and plants but those from abroad: balm, hyssop, Iceland moss, cinnamon, myrrh and aloes.

'I hope it succeeds,' she whispered, staring up at the candle wheel hanging from its pulley beneath the rafters. The shop would provide fresh sources of income. Perhaps she might increase her profits: she would buy her own field, certainly for the home-grown herbs and so remove the middleman. Kathryn leant against the counter, stroking the polished wood. But what would happen then? She had her patients, she was a city physician, so who would run the shop? Thomasina? Agnes? Colum? Kathryn smiled at the thought of the Irishman with an apron tied round his waist. He'd poison everyone within a month, she thought. Or should I continue as a physician?

'Daydreaming, Kathryn?' Thomasina stood in the doorway, her hands and wrists covered in flour.

'I was just thinking about the shop.'

Thomasina walked towards her. 'It will be a success,' her old nurse said. 'You are not really thinking of that, are you? It's the Irishman.'

Kathryn grinned. 'Well, yes and no. I went to that tavern.' Kathryn leaned against the counter. 'A terrible murder, Thomasina, in a nightmarish room. God knows if we will discover the murderer. And there's money involved, royal taxes.'

Thomasina made a rude sound with her mouth.

'But standing here in the shop,' Kathryn continued, 'listening to Wuf babble and play, I wondered whether I like these subtle, dark confrontations with some assassin.'

'And you haven't been to poor Blunt's house?' Thomasina asked.

'No, perhaps after we have eaten. Thomasina, you could help.'
'With Blunt?'
'Well, you know the story: Blunt returned home, slew his wife

and the two young men in dalliance. One tried to escape through a window but Blunt struck him with an arrow; the man fell out into the street, almost at the feet of Widow Gumple.'

'Oh, sweet Lord!' Thomasina groaned. 'Must she be involved?'

'Thomasina, I just want you to ask her: what precisely happened? Can you do that for me?'

Thomasina agreed. 'And the Irishman, Mistress? Is he going to stay here for the winter?'

Kathryn tapped Thomasina gently on the nose. 'Aye, Thomasina, and if God is good and I have my way, next winter too. Now, come. If I am not mistaken, our patients have arrived.'

Followed by a grumbling Thomasina, Kathryn hurried out of the shop. She went to her writing office, collected her herbarium and basket of jars and returned to the kitchen.

Thankfully, the list of ailments was minor. Two or three children with sore throats for which Kathryn prescribed a tincture of marjoram. Mollyns the miller also came, complaining he had a sore stomach.

'Too much ale,' Thomasina grumbled.

'Shut up!' the miller bawled back.

Kathryn calmed him down: she gave Mollyns an infusion of wild thyme and told him to take it after supper, in the morning and again at noon for the next week. The miller stomped off, looking blackly over his shoulder at Thomasina. The rest of the patients were mainly suffering from cuts and bruises. Hagar the washerwoman who had slipped on the ice and grazed her wrist and arm. She went away chattering thankfully for some witch hazel. Finally came Rawnose the beggar, who spent most of his time out in the open listening to and spreading gossip. He now had sore chilblains on his toes and fingers. Kathryn gave him the dried, crushed leaf buds of the black poplar.

'I can understand chilblains on your fingers,' she murdered. 'But you have good boots, Rawnose, and warm hose. And here's another pair.' She handed over an old pair of Colum's. 'So, how did you get chilblains on your toes?'

'I don't know,' Rawnose wailed, his poor, disfigured face still blue with the cold. 'I goes into the tavern, I gets the best place near the hearth, often the inglenook. Off comes my mittens, my boots and hose and I toast them in front of the fire.'

Kathryn pressed the herbal remedy into his hand, shouting for Agnes to bring a cup of warm posset. She remembered her father's warning about chilblains and, whilst Rawnose gratefully drank the hot spiced wine, Katryn tried to recall it.

'Is there anything wrong with this?' Rawnose asked, gesturing suspiciously at the little jar Kathryn had given him.

'Oh no,' Kathryn murmured. 'But the chilblains will come back.'

The beggar man, swathed in his rags, was almost out of the door, when Kathryn suddenly remembered.

'No, wait!' she cried. 'Rawnose, you say you go into the tavern and immediately warm your hands and toes before the fire?'

The beggar man scratched his face where his nose used to be.

'Oh yes, Mistress, I am always let through.'

Kathryn slipped a coin into his hand. 'In future, don't. If your hands are very cold and you hold them in front of the flames, the skin is chafed and some humour in the blood curdles.' She shook her head. 'I don't know why.'

'But I am freezing!' he wailed.

'Well,' Kathryn continued, 'first, try and restore the warmth naturally. Make sure your fingers and toes are fairly dry and warm, just for a few minutes, and you'll find the chilblains won't return.'

Rawnose looked in speechless admiration at this scat of wisdom.

'Are you sure, Mistress?' He shifted his gaze and Kathryn caught him looking longingly at the table.

'Are you hungry, Rawnose?'

The beggar man licked his lips wolfishly.

'Then stay for supper.'

Rawnose needed no second invitation. His rags came flying off and he sped like a greyhound to a stool in front of the fire.

'You'll wash your bloody hands!' Thomasina bellowed.

Rawnose trooped off to the scullery where Wuf and Agnes

helped him bathe his poor, chapped fingers. Colum came downstairs.

'Come on, woman!' he growled at Thomasina. 'Eat or be eaten!'

Kathryn cleared up the jars and bandages, washed her hands and took her place opposite Colum. Thomasina and Agnes served the meal. Kathryn said grace which she gabbled rather quickly because Rawnose's eyes were growing bigger and bigger at the sight of white loaves, pots of fragrant-smelling chicken and the large platter of vegetables cooked in a succulent sauce.

Thomasina and Agnes filled each person's bowl; Rawnose and Colum, with Wuf coming a good third, ate as if there was no tomorrow. Kathryn tapped her horn spoon on the table.

'The Greeks said that good digestion is a natural physic. Wuf, eat slowly.' Kathrynn winked at Colum. 'Do try and follow the example of others.'

Colum put his knife down. 'We must visit Blunt's house.'

'Poor man,' Rawnose intervened, his mouth full of chicken.

'Close your mouth when you are eating!' Thomasina snapped. Rawnose quickly obliged.

'What do the gossips say?' Kathryn asked.

Rawnose cleared his throat and shrugged. 'May should never marry December: old Blunt was infatuated with Alisoun. He ignored the advice of friends and his old housekeeper, Emma Darryl.'

'But to kill two men with a bow,' Agnes piped up.

'He was a master archer,' Thomasina interrupted. 'I knew Richard Blunt when he was a young man. He came from the shires with that feckless son of his and Emma his housekeeper.' She glanced at Kathryn. 'Your father liked him. In his day Richard Blunt was a merry soul and a fine dancer. He used to join the mummers on the green on May Day, sprightly-legged and bright-eyed.' She looked down at the platter. All gone, Thomasina thought, all those people of her youth: her husbands, their little children, her friends. Gone into the yawning grave and now Blunt, with his happy laugh and skilful arm, would hang for a harlot of a wife. Thomasina kept her head down. She felt the tears pricking her eyes but then glanced up and caught Wuf studying her sadly. She shifted on the bench.

'I am sorry,' she murmured. 'Sometimes the past makes its presence felt. God have mercy on Richard Blunt! Tell me, Kathryn,' Thomasina added, swiftly changing the conversation. 'The business at the Wicker Man?'

'I have heard about that as well,' Rawnose chortled. 'Dead as a nail old Erpingham is.'

'What do you think of the Smithlers?' Colum asked him.

Rawnose mumbled something but went back to his food.

'Wormhair,' Agnes said, her thin face full of importance.

'Wormhair your lover?' Wuf teased. 'I have seen him on the altar at St. Mildred's. Why won't his hair lie down?'

'Shush, Wuf,' Kathryn said. 'Agnes, you were saying?'

'Wormhair says the tavern is haunted.'

'I've heard that,' Thomasina declared, wiping her lips on her napkin. 'What truly happened there, Mistress?'

Kathryn, with an eye on both Rawnose and Wuf's attentive ears, briefly described Erpingham's death and the mystery surrounding it.

'It's the ghosts!' Rawnose portentously declared.

Kathryn glanced at Colum and raised her eyes heavenwards. By tomorrow, she thought, the story would be all over Canterbury.

There was a knock on the door and Agnes rushed to answer it. Kathryn's heart sank at the prospect of another visitor, but she relaxed as Luberon, a small beaver hat on his head and the bottom half of his face hidden by a great brown cloak, swept down the passageway. He came into the kitchen stamping his feet and shaking the drops of water from his cloak.

'I thought I'd best come,' he declared, staring fixedly at the chicken.

He, too, needed no second invitation. In the twinkling of an eye, his cloak had been taken off and Luberon squeezed himself between Thomasina and Agnes. He rubbed his hands gleefully as a bowl filled with succulent chicken was placed in front of him.

'We should open a tavern ourselves,' Colum remarked drily.

Luberon just smiled and nodded vigorously in agreement.

'I am not only here for your food,' he said after a few mouthfuls. 'I also bring information. The Wicker Man tavern may well be haunted. In 1235,' Luberon continued sonorously, 'in the reign of good Henry III, a priest fell in love with a lovely young woman from the city.' He glanced shrewdly at Kathryn. 'And, before you ask, the priest's name was Erpingham, Louis de Erpingham. He was, in fact, a canon of the cathedral who enjoyed a rather sinister reputation. A jury once accused Louis of dabbling in black magic and other Satanic rites but this was never proved. Anyway . . .' Luberon sighed, pleased he had everyone's attention. Rawnose in particular was all ears. The beggar man couldn't believe his good fortune at receiving treatment, obtaining new hose and a hearty supper, and now gleaning gossip which would keep him fed for at least a week.

'Anyway,' Luberon repeated, 'Louis fell in love with this young woman. God knows what happened but she was found dead one fine summer's day in the graveyard of Holy Cross Church. Suspicion immediately fell on Canon Louis de Erpingham. He went into hiding and tried to flee Canterbury in disguise. Now, you must remember, over two hundred years ago the Wicker Man stood well beyond the city walls. Louis de Erpingham apparently stayed there and, whether he fell into a fit of melancholy or was frightened of being captured, hanged himself in the very chamber where our tax collector was murdered.'

'Did Sir Reginald belong to the same family?' Colum asked.

'Possibly,' Luberon replied. 'He may have been attracted to that chamber because of some ghoulish memory about his ancestor. Whatever, there are records which show that, time and again in the past two hundred years since Louis's death, both the tavern and that chamber in particular have been reported as haunted. Strange manifestations, movements at night, putrid smells, eerie cries; common gossip claims it's the ghost of the hanged priest. The place has been exorcised but, as the years roll by, the legends continue to flourish.' Luberon sipped from his wine goblet generously filled by Thomasina who sat fascinated by this juicy morsel of city history.

'So,' Kathryn leaned back in her chair. 'An Erpingham hanged himself at the Wicker Man over two hundred years ago. Now Sir Reginald is found poisoned in the same chamber.'

'Do you think our dead tax collector knew all this?' Colum asked.

'Perhaps,' Kathryn said. 'Erpingham was a sinister man but he was also a trained clerk and lawyer. He could have read the same manuscript as Master Luberon did.'

'And the ghost?' Colum asked. 'No, don't laugh at me, Kathryn. True, I am Irish, born and bred on legends about the undead, the banshees.' Colum glanced away. 'But sometimes, the stories . . .'

'What stories?' Wuf cried.

'Once,' Colum replied before Kathryn could stop him, 'I lived in a village where there was an evil old woman. On a night like this, when the snow had fallen thick and fast, she knocked on the door of my house.'

'That's not frightening,' Wuf said.

'Oh, yes it was. You see, I went back to tell my father this old witch had called and he became all afeared, pale with fright. He ran to the door and opened it but the old crone was gone.'

'Why was he frightened?' Kathryn asked curiously.

'Because,' Colum replied in a sepulchral tone, 'earlier that day the old woman had died. I didn't believe him, I'd seen her! But then my father pointed to the unbroken snow and, of course, demons and ghosts leave no footprints.'

'Nonsense!' Thomasina trumpeted.

'I don't know,' Colum said. 'Sometimes such things happen. Anyway, Master Luberon, what else did you discover?'

'Well, I found Sir Reginald's house in St. Alphage's Lane.'

'And?'

'All locked, barred and bolted: it will be worth a visit in the morning.' Luberon sipped from his goblet. 'I discovered nothing else about Erpingham, though the city archives did reveal a great deal about Master Blunt. Apparently he told lies.'

'Such as?' Kathryn asked.

'Well, the common account says he came from Warwickshire with his housekeeper Emma Darryl and the witless Peter, his son by his first wife.'

'And?' Kathryn prompted.

'Well, one of the gaolers of the guildhall, when asked by Blunt if there was any news, mentioned the gossip concerning Erpingham's death at the Wicker Man. On hearing this, Blunt began to laugh, becoming almost frenetic, coughing and spluttering until the gaoler thought he would suffer an apoplexy. The gaoler asked him why he found such news so amusing and Blunt made the startling confession that he and Master Erpingham knew each other well.' Luberon closed his eyes to marshal his thoughts; he felt tired and sleepy after his walk through the snow and the hearty meal he had just eaten. 'Yes, that's it. Blunt explained how years earlier, Erpingham had tried to take his head.'

'Take his head?' Colum repeated. 'But that's the legal term used for killing an outlaw. Yes, Wuf, before you ask, an outlaw is called a wolf-head because, like a wolf, he can be killed on sight.'

'I reflected on this,' Luberon continued. 'So I searched the city archives and discovered that, in his younger days, Erpingham had been a royal official, a verderer in the Weald of Kent. He had the specific task of tracking down outlaws, Blunt in particular.'

Kathryn cupped her chin in her hands and stared down at Colum.

'Do you think all these murders are connected?' she asked.

Colum got to his feet, pushing back his chair. 'As they say in Ireland, all roads, however twisted, will eventually take you to your destination.'

'What?' Kathryn exclaimed. 'No quotation from Chaucer?'

'I can think of one,' Colum joked back. ' "Satan, who ever waits men to beguile." Well, he certainly has me beguiled. Come on,' he urged. 'Master Luberon, Mistress Kathryn, the day is not yet done. You want to visit Blunt's house, so let's not tarry.'

Kathryn collected her cloak and changed her buskins for wool-lined boots. She gave instructions to Thomasina and warned Wuf to be good. Then she, Colum and Luberon walked out into the black, icy night.

Colum, now rested and well fed, was in fine fettle, pointing up to the starlit skies.

'I told you,' he exclaimed. 'The weather is breaking. See, Kathryn, by morning time it will be warmer and the thaw will be with us.'

'Thank God!' Luberon breathed. 'A dreadful sight was reported today: some poor vagrant, drunk or tired, stumbled into a ditch last night just outside Westgate. They discovered his corpse this morning, still standing upright, frozen as a statue.' Luberon pushed his way between Kathryn and Colum. 'I suppose things are no better at Kingsmead?'

Colum blew his breath out then watched it hang in the icy night air. 'No, some provisions are being brought in and the horses are stabled, but the work on the manor house will have to wait.'

They turned out of Ottemelle Lane into Steward Street. The night was pitch black except for the lantern horns hanging outside the merchants' houses and the chinks of light glinting through gaps in the shutters. Somewhere a dog howled mournfully at the winter moon and hungry cats scavenged fruitlessly amongst the frozen mounds of refuse. They passed a tavern door, slightly open. The noise, smell and laughter seeping out seemed strange in that cold, deserted street. Kathryn and her companions walked on, more concerned with keeping a secure footing, well away from the sewer that ran along the street; this had frozen hard, though here and there the ice was beginning to break.

At last they entered Church Lane and the spire of St. Mildred's came into view, illuminated by the great lantern hanging in its tower.

'Blunt lived in an alleyway on the far side,' Luberon remarked.

'We'll only visit there tonight,' Kathryn declared, her teeth chattering with the cold. 'Whatever secrets Master Erpingham's secret house held will just have to wait.'

Luberon stopped, shuffling his feet in embarrassment. Kathryn beat her gloved hands together.

'Come on, Simon, it's too cold to dally. What is it?'

The clerk cleared his throat. 'It's not only the scene of the crime we have to visit,' he muttered, his head and face hidden by the cowl. 'But Master Murtagh is the King's coroner and you are his physician. You must also view the corpses.'

Kathryn closed her eyes and groaned; Colum cursed loudly in Gaelic.

'Lord, man!' he bellowed. 'Haven't we seen enough dead bodies for one day?'

Kathryn linked one arm through Colum's, the other through Luberon's.

'We'll view them,' she said. 'I suppose they are to be buried tomorrow?'

Luberon nodded.

'And have you had further thoughts on Erpingham's death?' he asked quickly. 'I didn't want to question you back at the house.'

Kathryn stared across the walls of St. Mildred's frozen cemetery.

'No, it's a mystery. But I tell you this. The Wicker Man tavern holds a great many secrets and I do fear for those who shelter there!'

Chapter 6

Blunt's was a narrow dwelling standing on the corner of an alleyway under the looming mass of St. Mildred's Church. Kathryn pointed farther along the alleyway.

'That's where one of the victims fell. I wonder what Widow Gumple was doing there at that time of night?' She looked up at the front of the house. 'My father told me a great deal about the city history. This house is probably hundreds of years old, with the solarium on the first floor, its windows along the side.'

'Well, I'm freezing!' Colum groaned, hammering on the door.

They heard footsteps and a woman's voice hoarsely asked who was there. Luberon explained; chains and bolts were loosened and the door swung open. The woman who stood there grasped a cane, her small, plump body covered in a shabby cloak, a mass of grey, wiry hair falling down to her shoulders; strong-faced and keen-eyed, she had an aquiline nose, thin lips and a determined chin.

'You are Emma Darryl?' Luberon asked.

'Of course I am!' the woman replied. 'You must be Master Luberon. We have met before: your companions are the King's coroner, the Irishman Murtagh and, of course, Mistress Swinbrooke.' She smiled faintly at Kathryn. 'You probably don't remember me but I knew your father well, a good man. I was sorry to hear of his death.'

Kathryn thanked her.

'Well, come in.'

Kathryn and the rest followed her in. The small hallway was bleak but smelt sweet. Kathryn glimpsed the precious herbs in the pots around the wall as Emma led them up the narrow, rickety stairs. At the top was a small gallery to the right and a door leading to the solarium. Emma ushered them in. Kathryn was surprised at the solarium's spaciousness and realised how deceptive the exterior of the house looked. The chamber was pleasantly furnished. Some canvas paintings hung against the walls. A pine log fire crackled merrily in the cavernous hearth of the fireplace, under a canopied mantelpiece shaped in the form of a bishop's mitre. At the far end, under the shuttered window, was a large embrasure with cushioned seats. Tables, chairs and quilted stools were tastefully arranged around the room with large, steel-bound chests placed against the wall. The floor at the entrance to the solarium was strewn with rushes, clean, dry and sprinkled with herbs. The rest of the floor was of polished wood and covered by thick woollen rugs. Two chairs stood before the fireplace, in one of which a young man lolled, staring vacuously into the flames. Emma Darryl caught his sharp glance.

'Yes, it happened here,' she declared. 'But come, Peter, we have guests.'

The young man in front of the fire rose, rather lopsidedly, and shambled towards them. He was thickset, his vacuous face fringed by a mop of dullish red hair. A slight line of spittle drooled from one corner of his mouth and his childlike eyes were still red-rimmed from crying. He mumbled a greeting, shaking each of their hands and made a clumsy attempt to kiss the back of Kathryn's. She smiled back as she felt his slack grip. For a few moments there was confusion as Peter, grunting and mumbling, pulled other chairs up around the fire whilst Emma brought them small cups of hippocras from the kitchen farther down the outside gallery. Colum tried to make conversation with Peter as

Emma Darryl scurried backwards and forwards and Kathryn studied the chamber more closely. She half closed her eyes; young Alisoun must have been sitting where she was, teasing and flirting with those two men. Richard Blunt would have come in through the doorway, arrows already notched. Kathryn had seen master bowmen in action and knew how fast and accurate their delivery was. Alisoun and one young man, perhaps fuddled with drink, died immediately; the other tried to reach the window, scrabbling at the shutter. He would open that and the casement beyond. Yes, Kathryn reflected, he'd have had time to do that, but as he climbed through, Blunt followed, firing straight into his back. Death would have been instantaneous for all three victims. The longbow arrow was at least a yard long, steel-tipped, its path guided by the grey goose feathers, and the power of the longbow could put such an arrow through a knight in full armour. Colum turned and glanced at her.

'Inquisitive as ever, Kathryn?' he smiled. 'Yes, it could be done. The three victims would have been in their cups, lounging about.' He pointed to the candles placed around the solarium. 'And there's enough light for even the weakest marksman.'

He paused as Emma returned; she sat down next to Peter, cradling his hands in her lap.

'Have you seen Master Blunt?' Emma asked.

'No,' Kathryn replied. 'I apologise but we were distracted by the death of Sir Reginald Erpingham at the Wicker Man. You have heard the news?'

Emma nodded.

'Did you know Erpingham?'

'No.' Emma's answer was too short, too quick, though the housekeeper stared coolly back at Kathryn. 'I understand he was a wicked man,' she continued. 'And certainly deserved his fate, unlike Master Blunt.'

'How long have you known the painter?' Colum asked.

'Thirty years.'

Kathryn stared at the woman. She looked plain and rather submissive but Kathryn sensed an inner strength.

'And, before you ask, Mistress Kathryn,' Emma said, 'I served

Master Blunt because he is a good man. He cared for me. I was a foundling and where else could I go? He was also a gifted painter. He should never have married that harlot Alisoun.' She spat the last words out so venomously that Kathryn knew, whatever Emma Darryl said, that she was deeply in love with Richard Blunt.

Kathryn straightened in her chair and put the goblet down on the floor beside her.

'Mistress Daryl, before we continue, let me tell you what we know. Master Blunt did not come from Warwickshire. I suspect he was born here in Kent, somewhere near Rochester. A gifted young man, he probably ran wild in his youth, perhaps a little poaching in the forests and along the Weald of Kent. In doing so, he became an outlaw. Moreover, before he either changed his name or accepted the King's pardon, Blunt was hunted by a verderer called Reginald Erpingham, who was later knighted, becoming the King's principal tax collector in the shire.' Kathryn gently raised her hand as Emma opened her mouth. 'No, Blunt has already confessed to this.'

The housekeeper leaned back in the chair, rocking herself gently.

'You are correct,' she sighed. 'My master's real name was Ralph Sockler, an outlaw; he killed three of the old king's deer and led Erpingham a merry dance. Eventually Blunt fled. He took service with the Earl of Warwick and went with him.' Emma gave a laugh and clenched the young man's hand even more firmly. 'No more lies. Blunt was not married to anyone before Alisoun: this boy is mine as well as his.'

'So Blunt refused to marry you?' Kathryn asked.

The housekeeper shook her head. 'No, I refused to marry him. Why hold a man down for a night of passion? And lose everything in a life of recrimination? I suppose Blunt loved me, we certainly saw the days. We were on the last ship out of Calais when the war ended. We settled in Canterbury, thinking the past had forgotten us.'

'And Erpingham?' Colum asked.

'Last summer he met Blunt by accident in the Buttermarket

and immediately challenged him.' Emma paused and looked at the young man's face but Peter sat in his chair like a dutiful child, not comprehending what was really going on.

'And Erpingham threatened Master Blunt?'

'I think he did more than that, Mistress Swinbrooke. On a number of occasions he came to the house. The master always saw him by himself; I think Sir Reginald was not above black-mail.'

'Did you or your master approach Erpingham at the Wicker Man?' Colum asked.

The housekeeper grimaced. 'No, but Erpingham summoned us there. He sent Blunt a letter saying when he would arrive; he gave him the date and advised that he could settle his account.'

'In other words, pay blackmail?'

'Of course, but Blunt refused to go.'

Emma stooped and threw another log on the fire. 'Isn't it strange,' she murmured as if to herself, 'how matters unfold? There was poor Richard worrying about Erpingham and, all the time, his sweet little wife was playing the weasel with any hand-some young man.'

'You knew this?' Kathryn asked.

'Everyone in Canterbury did, apart from him. She had a fire in her loins, did Alisoun. She married Richard for his money and, until she appeared, he had good silver banked with the gold-smiths.'

'And Master Blunt was totally ignorant of Alisoun's dal-liances?' Kathryn asked.

'Oh, he might have suspected but he turned a blind eye, becoming engrossed in his beloved paintings.'

'And what happened the night Alisoun died?'

The old housekeeper glanced at the fire, rubbing the side of her face.

'I don't really know,' she murmured. 'Richard and Peter had been finishing a painting in St. Mildred's. They arrived home late, having stopped at a tavern. No, not the Wicker Man, though Blunt was still worried about Erpingham's threats. Now the snow was falling, lying thick and fast, so Blunt hurried home, sending Peter ahead to see if the bakery was still open.' She looked round, tears welling in her eyes. 'I knew what was going on. I have my chamber on the top floor, but what could I do? If I told the master, he would just reply that Alisoun was young and perhaps needed the company of people of her own age. If I remonstrated with the harlot . . .' The housekeeper trailed off and scratched her head. 'Well, she may have had a pretty face and a sweet mouth, but Alisoun could curse like any soldier.' Emma stopped to dab at her eyes. 'She threatened that if I said anything to the master, I'd be dismissed.'

'But would he have done that?' Kathryn asked.

'Alisoun had a sweet, soft and supple body: between the sheets she would have enthralled any man.'

'Continue,' Kathryn asked; she glimpsed the hurt and pain in the old woman's eyes. 'We must know,' Kathryn whispered. 'For God's sake, Mistress Darryl, three people died that night.'

'Will Daddy come home?' The young man suddenly spoke up in a thin, shrill voice. He looked wide-eyed at Kathryn. 'We haven't finished the painting yet. I'm glad Alisoun's gone. She would laugh at me and nip my arm. Once she even tripped me so I fell downstairs.' The poor witless lad stared around. 'Daddy has to come. Soon it will be Yuletide.'

'Shush now, boy!' Emma stroked his hand gently and smiled apologetically at Kathryn. 'He's all a-fey tonight. I think he suspects: usually he is better than this.' She put one arm protectively round the young man's shoulders. He now sat rocking, backwards and forwards, his thumb firmly in his mouth.

'It was over so quickly,' Emma continued in a matter-of-fact voice. 'Master Blunt came home; he must have come up the stairs quietly, taking his boots off because of the snow. He pushed the door open and . . .' She chewed the corner of her lip. 'Richard was a gentle man, but in his youth he had been both hot-tempered and a master bowman. I have seen him shoot six arrows into a target in less than a minute. I doubt if Alisoun or her companions knew what was happening. The first I heard was the clatter of the window shutters and the young man screaming whilst he tried to escape. I put on a robe and hurried down.' Emma shrugged. 'The rest you know.'

Kathryn just stared at her.

'The master looked terrible,' Emma continued. 'Just standing in the doorway, the bow in his hand, the quiver at his feet. Alisoun lay before the hearth, her bodice untied, an arrow in her throat. The young man had taken the other straight in the heart. I heard the shouting and screaming from the alley below. Peter came back, then the bailiffs.' She drew her breath in sharply. 'I have no more to add.' She withdrew her arm from Peter and put her face in her hands, sobbing gently.

Kathryn crouched beside her, clasping her hand.

'What can we do?' The housekeeper looked up, her face tear-stained. 'What should I do, Mistress?'

Kathryn shook her head. 'Do you need anything?'

'No.' Emma wiped her eyes with the back of her hand. 'Just visit the master. Tell him all is well. See what comfort you can give.'

They left a few minutes later. Colum was visibly uncomfortable at what he had witnessed; Luberon hid his face in his cowl, though Kathryn glimpsed the clerk dabbing at his eyes. Colum stared up at the starlit sky and moved Kathryn and Luberon gently away from the houses and the icy snow that was threatening to fall from their roofs.

'God have mercy on them all!' he whispered, looking down at Kathryn. 'What can we do?'

'Nothing,' she replied. 'He killed three people. There's nothing under heaven we can do for Richard Blunt.'

'Alisoun was a bitch,' Luberon added. 'God save us, that could be any one of us. But come.'

He led them round St. Mildred's Church, through the lychgate and across the deserted frozen cemetery. They stumbled along the winding path between the lopsided crosses and battered headstones. All around them was a frozen stillness; not even a nightjar or hunting owl broke the silence of the graveyard, buried under its carpet of white snow.

'Just follow me!' Luberon called over his shoulder. 'I had this path cleared.'

He stopped and pointed into the darkness. 'They'll be buried here. Though the graves will be shallow, the soil's iron hard. Perhaps in spring we can dig deeper . . .' Luberon's voice faltered and he led them on.

Outside the death house, a small brick building that stood next to the cemetery wall within easy walking distance of the death door in the side of the church, Luberon stopped and took out a tinder. After a great deal of scraping, he lit the two lantern horns hanging over the entrance. He handed one of these to Colum, unlocked the door and took them in. Kathryn had never been in a room so cold and bleak. Luberon also lit the cresset torches but even their light and the incense bowl, which had been lit and placed in a thurible hanging on the wall, did nothing to hide the smell of death and the stench of putrefaction. Three pinewood coffins rested next to one another on a long trestle table. Luberon drew his dagger and loosened the coffin lids. Then he pulled back the black palls and white gauze sheets underneath, gesturing at Colum and Kathryn to come forward. At first Kathryn just stared in horror at these three young people. If it had not been for the greenish-white tinge of their skin, which looked even more ghoulish in the torchlight, and the waxen texture of their flesh, they could have been sleeping. She touched Alisoun's arm. In life the young woman must have been beautiful; blond hair, like burnished gold, framed a pretty oval face with regular features. The young men were thickset and well built. Kathryn pitied the cruel fate which had shattered their lives as well as that of Richard Blunt.

'The embalmers have been busy,' Luberon whispered. He coughed apologetically. 'I was wrong—they are not to be buried tomorrow but first given to the care of their relatives, though I think the men will be buried here, at least until spring when the roads are more passable.'

'What is it?' Colum hissed at Kathryn, busy with the corpses.

Despite his military service, Colum was afraid. These unlidded caskets, the ghoulish corpses in the flickering torchlight, the deathly silence of this cold shed and, outside, nothing but the white stillness. The Irishman recalled the stories of his youth and the great wakes he had attended in the villages outside Dublin. He remembered how the old ones used to whisper that the dead never journey direct to God but lurk in the shadows to make their sad farewells to the land of the living. Colum stared into one darkened corner. Did the ghost of the beautiful Alisoun stand there? He jumped and cursed as a rat scurried under the table and disappeared out of the door.

'For God's sake!' he snapped. 'What is the matter?'

Kathryn was now feeling the skin of each corpse. She lifted the grave clothes Alisoun lay in and ran her hand gently across the dead woman's stomach. She ignored Colum's question.

'Master Luberon, can I see the wounds?'

Luberon stepped back, his face deathly pale as he clutched his stomach.

'Do what you want,' he replied thickly. 'I think the night air may be best for me.'

Colum would have joined him, but Kathryn seized him by the wrist.

'Come, Irishman,' Kathryn murmured. 'There's no ghost or banshee here. Help me to turn them over.'

Colum gritted his teeth, half closed his eyes and obeyed. He just thanked God he was wearing gloves and didn't have to feel the corpses against his skin. Kathryn, however, remained impassive.

'Undoubtedly arrow wounds,' she commented and pointed to the purple-ringed gash in the chest of one of the young men. 'But such great force!'

'I've seen an arrow go straight through a man,' Colum said. 'Why, Kathryn, is there anything wrong?'

Kathryn pointed to the ragged hole in Alisoun's throat.

'Oh, for heaven's sake, Colum, look!'

Colum stared down. The wound was large, the flesh scarcely torn.

'Blunt caught her straight,' he observed. 'Perhaps she was coming towards him?'

Kathryn rearranged the corpses and, with Colum's help, drew back the veils and black woollen cloths, then resealed the coffin.

'I have seen enough,' she whispered. 'Time will tell, time will tell!'

And, remaining enigmatic, she went outside where she picked up a lump of snow and carefully washed her hands with it.

'You can douse the lights, Simon,' she called, her voice ringing like a bell across the bleak white cemetery.

Luberon hastened to obey.

'Well.' Kathryn came between the clerk and Colum, linking her hands through their arms. 'You, Colum, the King's coroner, can record that all are indeed dead and undoubtedly murdered. Master Luberon, you can complete the necessary documents.' She looked across at the yew trees which, standing stark and black in the silvery moonlight, took on a horrid, almost lifelike stance as if they were some dreadful creatures from hell, frozen by the winter cold.

'Come on,' she said. 'I have had enough of graves and graveyards for one night.'

'Was there anything wrong?' Colum asked as they left by the wicket gate.

'Time will tell,' Kathryn said again. 'But now, do we retire to our beds or visit Sir Reginald Erpingham's secret house in St. Alphage's Lane?'

'Lord, what o'clock is it?' Luberon asked, stamping his feet against the cold.

'God knows!' Colum replied. 'All the bells are silent.' He looked up at the stars. 'But it has been dark for some hours. I would reckon between nine and ten o'clock.'

'Let's go to St. Alphage's Lane,' Kathryn insisted. 'I am intrigued by what Erpingham may have kept there.'

'What are the possibilities?' Luberon asked as they walked back up to Ottemelle Lane. 'I mean, about Erpingham's death?'

Kathryn blew her breath out. She watched it hang in the cold night air: like steam, she thought, from a boiling pot. Why did it do that? She recalled her father's fierce debate with his colleagues about whether the human breath could carry contagion. If it did,

Kathryn thought absent-mindedly, would the cold night air kill it or make it stronger?

Colum suddenly slipped on a piece of ice and all three of them steadied themselves, laughing and joking but lapsing into silence as they passed Kathryn's house. Once they'd entered St. Margaret's Street, however, Luberon returned to his questioning about Erpingham.

'I'm still puzzled,' Kathryn admitted flatly. 'Here we have a tax collector who eats and drinks the same as everyone else. He goes upstairs to his chamber, carrying a goblet of untainted wine. The only person to follow him is old Gervase. The rest also disperse, and Standon takes up guard at the foot of the stairs. The next morning Erpingham is dead. No trace of any poison, no sign of any murderer visiting him, the window and door of his chamber both locked and bolted. We know everyone hated him. Some are quite candid—they wished him dead, but there's no evidence of their involvement in his murder.'

'The chamber was haunted,' Colum added, his mood still affected by his recent visit to the macabre death house.

'Oh, yes, I can see that,' Kathryn replied, staring up at the houses on either side. 'Erpingham was a godless man, fascinated by anything sinister or macabre. He may have well been proud that an ancestor died in that chamber. However, according to the old knight, when Erpingham had his nightmare he was truly terrified.'

Kathryn and her two companions paused as a group of hooded, ragged figures slipped out of Hawk Lane and shuffled towards them. Kathryn quickly counted five or six figures. They moved slowly, carrying staves, their leader holding up a paltry lantern.

'Have pity!' his voice whined. 'Oh, good Christians, have pity!'

Colum's hand fell to his sword hilt. The group drew nearer. Kathryn caught a strange, sour smell, but as the leader approached, one of the group beat two hollow sticks together, followed by the tinkle of a bell and the cry 'Unclean! Unclean!'

'By Maeve's teats!' Colum grasped his sword. 'Lepers!'

Luberon scuttled into the entrance of a doorway.

The leper leader stopped before Kathryn and raised his head. Kathryn's heart lurched in both fear and compassion. The man's face was completely eaten away: a bloody stain marked his nose; one eye was closed by a growth high on his right cheek and the terrible disease had begun to eat into his lower jaw. The man stretched out one maimed hand.

'We are so cold,' he rasped. 'Oh, for sweet Christ's sake!'

Kathryn dipped into her purse; she thought again and emptied its contents into the man's hands.

'Go back down Hawk Lane,' she said. 'At the far end, across the street, you will see a large building like a church.' She paused, staring at the man's one good eye. 'Knock on the door, speak to the priest, Father Cuthbert. There's a shelter behind the hospital. Say Mistress Swinbrooke sent you.'

'Aye, and Colum Murtagh, the King's Commissioner.' The Irishman, now embarrassed by his fear, came back.

The leper raised one hand and, turning slowly, led his disfigured companions back into the darkness.

Luberon waddled out of his hiding place.

'I am sorry. Mistress, truly I am, but they terrify me.'

Kathryn squeezed him by the arm. 'Simon, I would be just as terrified, but my father told me that leprosy is not infectious, not unless you bathe, eat, drink and sleep with them.'

She stood at the corner of Hawk Lane and watched the dark shapes disappear down the alleyway between the overhanging houses. The clatter of their rattle and the chime of the silver bell sounded eerie in the frozen stillness. Kathryn did not move. For some strange reason she thought of her absent husband, Alexander Wyville. What if he was sick or ill like this? Or even travelling in disguise?

'Come on, Kathryn!' Colum urged.

They continued up the deserted street past St. Margaret's Church and across the Mercery. Canterbury seemed like some ghost city; even the great tavern, the Chequer of Hope, had its lights dimmed and windows boarded. Nothing moved on the street except scavenging cats, though now and again Kathryn glimpsed dark shadows in doorways and, on the corners of alleyways, beggars or highwaymen desperate for any business. They passed the bull-stake that marked the end of the Buttermarket. Some travellers congregated there, seeking shelter at the Sun Inn, a large tavern near Christchurch Gate. Above this loomed the soaring, crenellated, foursquare towers of the cathedral, stretching up as if to touch the starlit sky. The stocks and whipping posts outside Christchurch Gate were empty.

'The courts are not busy,' Luberon said.

'They will be soon,' Colum added. 'It will get warmer. By morning, the thaw will have arrived and the Lord help anyone who has a hole in their roof.'

'Those guests will remain at the Wicker Man?' Kathryn asked.

'Oh, yes,' Colum replied. 'They must.'

'I'm trying to imagine,' Luberon intervened, 'what Erpingham would have done when he reached his chamber. We know he went up alone, carrying a goblet of wine. He apparently locked and bolted the door. He then undressed, probably sipping from his wine. What else would he do?'

Kathryn paused and clutched Luberon's wrist. 'Oh, most subtle clerk,' she breathed. 'Of course! But that only deepens the mystery.'

'What does?' Colum asked.

'Irishman, what would you do if you were a tax official and the silver you had collected was in saddlebags left in your locked room? Now, you'd been absent supping belowstairs and then you return?'

'I'd check the saddlebags,' Colum replied.

'And if they were empty?' Kathryn continued. 'You'd immediately run out and raise the alarm. Accordingly,' Kathryn concluded, 'when Erpingham retired to bed that night, the silver must have still been in those saddlebags unless, of course, Erpingham's mind was on other matters. But what?'

None of her companions could answer. They walked under the great towering mass of the cathedral; after Turn Again Lane they crossed Sun Street and went down St. Alphage's Lane. This was as dark as pitch and Luberon had some difficulty in remembering where Erpingham's house stood, but at last they found it: a narrow, two-storied tenement that looked as if it had been pushed in between the houses on either side. Luberon handed Kathryn the keys; she opened the front door and they entered the stone-flagged hallway. Colum struck a tinder, lit a rushlight and then went deeper into the house looking for candles. At last he returned carrying some and they began their search.

The house was very small: a kitchen, a small parlour on the ground floor and, on the narrow gallery above, a small empty garret beside an opulently furnished bedchamber. As they lit more candles, Kathryn and Colum marvelled at the comfort and wealth of Erpingham's little hideaway. The bedchamber was hung with cloths, rugs covered the floor and a copper-gilt brazier stood in every corner. Bronze candleholders were fastened to the wall. The bed itself was costly: the tester and counterpane of the great four-poster were of silken cloth fringed with silver tassels. The long bolster was featherdown, its covering matching the sheets of smooth red samite. Downstairs in the kitchen, bronze pots and pewter cups stood neatly on shelves. On either side of a small baker's hearth, fleshing knives, skillets and ladles, all washed and polished, hung from shining hooks on the wall. The small parlour was no different: wooden panelling covered the walls even above the small, canopied hearth. Box chairs, their seats quilted, stood in every corner; woollen rugs were strewn on the floor. A polished, oval table, with high-backed chairs on either side, stood in the centre of the room.

'A little love nest,' Colum declared. 'I have seen the like before, maintained by great noblemen or royal officials. Erpingham must have been a wealthy man to own this house for such infrequent visits. I wager he was well known to the ladies of the town or to any woman who fell into his evil clutches.'

'There's a coffer under the table,' Luberon exclaimed, squatting down and pointing.

Colum pulled this out. It was about two yards long, metal-studded and reinforced with iron bands. It had three locks but none of the keys Kathryn carried fitted. Colum returned to the kitchen and came back with a hammer; he roughly smashed the locks open, throwing back the lid.

A sweet fragrant smell filled the room. Kathryn pulled out the bag of herbs, a small book covered in calfskin and other scraps of parchment. She opened the book. At first, because of its brilliant colours, she thought it was a Book of Hours but then she studied the paintings carefully and smiled. She passed it to Colum.

'No prayer book,' she murmured. 'Each page depicts a lovely young lady, in a number of poses, naked as the day she was born.'

Colum fairly snatched it from her hands as Kathryn began to study the scraps of parchment. She put her hand back into the chest.

'And there's more!'

Kathryn pulled out small pouches and then the yellowing skull of a dog, a cross with a dried bat crucified upside down on it, a mandrake root and balls of wax. Kathryn stared in disgust at these tools and devices of black magic and threw them back into the empty coffer.

'Let's leave,' she said, studying the pieces of parchment before putting them into her wallet.

Colum and Luberon agreed. They made one last search of the house but could find no other coffer or secret compartment. Luberon promised he would return the following morning to make a second sweep. Kathryn nodded absent-mindedly. She had scrutinized the scraps of parchment carefully, especially the drawing of a huge wicker man, similar to the painting on the sign of the tavern where Erpingham had died. A giant built of twigs and branches, and inside it, sets of initials which Kathryn had immediately recognised.

Chapter 7

Kathryn slept late the following morning, and when she got out of bed and pulled back the shutters of her window, she laughed.

'Trust an Irishman!'

The sun had risen and a strong thaw had arrived. On the roof-tops across Ottemelle Lane, the snow was already beginning to slide down to the eaves and Kathryn could hear the water dripping from the gable end of her own house. Kathryn opened the casement, breathed in the ice-cold air and listened to the clatter of the carts and the shouts from the street below. The city would make up for lost time; the early morning mist was already being burnt off and, through the clear morning air, above the rattle of the carts, the crack of whips and the cries of the early morning traders, Kathryn heard the great bells of the cathedral tolling for morning Mass. She shivered, closed the window and quickly washed and dressed. Kathryn then lit the hour candle, trimming it carefully with a knife so the flame began at the tenth red circle. From the cathedral bells Kathryn knew it must be about two hours before noon. She dabbed a little of her precious ointment on her neck and the palms of her hands, then pulled back the bedspread, stripping off the sheets and bolster covers: Thomasina would wash the bedding and take advantage of the change in the weather.

'Kathryn! Kathryn!' Wuf jumped up and down outside in the gallery.

She opened the door and the little boy thrust a wooden disc in her face.

'I've carved it myself!' he declared. 'I can use it on the ice!'

Kathryn patted his head absent-mindedly and said good morning to Agnes; the maid was already taking a bundle of sheets down to the small washhouse that stood in the far corner of the garden.

In the kitchen below, Thomasina was preparing a pot of steaming oatmeal over the fire. The old nurse straightened up and looked at her sternly. 'You were long gone yesterday evening!'

Kathryn smiled. 'Coroner's business, Thomasina!' She stared up at the newly baked bread Thomasina had hauled up so it swung from just below the rafters, well away from any foraging mice. 'That smells sweet.'

'Don't change the subject!' Thomasina snapped. 'What were you and that bloody Irishman up to?'

Kathryn walked over. 'He seized me, Thomasina,' she whispered. 'Dragged me up an alleyway and cruelly ravished me.'

Thomasina stuck her tongue out. 'It's wrong to tell lies.' She turned away to stir the oatmeal. 'But even as a child you were fanciful.'

Kathryn made a face and sat down at the table. She and Colum had walked back from Erpingham's house. They had not talked about what they had found, Colum undergoing one of his abrupt changes of mood. He'd pointed to the stars and begun to recount his youthful exploits as a boy in Ireland.

'The sky is very clear there,' he'd commented. 'I used to go out and sing songs. They say it's lucky to sing to the stars: the ancients claim that when the stars move and the planets whirl, the heavens are full of music.'

And without any invitation from Kathryn, Colum had begun to sing a lilting, bittersweet Gaelic song. Kathryn smiled to herself.

'Here's your oatmeal!' Thomasina slammed the bowl down in front of her. 'And your milk and there's your honey. Now, if you are going to sit like a cat who has stolen the cream, that's fine by me!' Thomasina walked away, her back as stiff as a poker.

Kathryn poured the milk and scooped a lump of honey. She put it over the oatmeal and began to sip carefully.

'And there's your ale.' Thomasina thrust a flagon of watered ale along the table.

Kathryn put the horn spoon down.

'Thomasina, come here.'

Her old nurse flounced across and Kathryn grabbed her hand.

'We walked home,' Kathryn declared, 'under the stars. Colum sang a song for me. Thomasina, can you blame us? Murder, heartbreak, the viewing of corpses at the dead of night: unravelling the mystery of Erpingham.'

Thomasina's face softened. 'Just be careful,' she pleaded. 'Do you still want me to see Widow Gumple?'

'No,' Kathryn replied.

Thomasina glanced away, closed her eyes and murmured a prayer of thanks. She despised Widow Gumple with all her heart. Not only did she regard the good widow as an arrogant hypocrite, but months earlier Thomasina had trapped Widow Gumple into confessing she had been sending blackmail letters to her mistress, taunting her about the whereabouts of Alexander Wyville. Thomasina smiled to herself: the letters had stopped though God only knew the whereabouts of Alexander Wyville.

'How were the Blunts?' Thomasina asked.

'Emma Darryl is a strong woman,' Kathryn said between mouthfuls. 'Peter is still in some sort of trance. Colum and I intend to visit Richard later in the day.'

Thomasina went back to stir the oatmeal. She absent-mindedly stirred the food, watching the creamy mixture turn like butter in a churn. All things pass, Thomasina thought sadly. Kathryn had changed since the Irishman's arrival: she was more resolute and determined. Murtagh had given her a new lease on life: Kathryn had used her sharp observation and acute mind to trap a number of murderers. After her success at the castle earlier in the year, even the King had sent a purse of gold and a personal letter of thanks 'TO HIS DEAR AND FAVOURED PHYSICIAN, KATHRYN SWIN-BROOKE, DWELLING IN OTTEMELLE LANE.' Nevertheless, the tragedy of the Blunt household had sharpened Thomasina's sense of time passing and life changing. She had always had a soft spot for the painter with his dancing eyes and merry smile. Now he'd hang on the gibbet set up in the Buttermarket. He would dance those dreadful steps as the rope strangled his breath. A vague idea took firmer shape in Thomasina's mind.

'Can I come?' she asked over her shoulder.

'Come where?' Colum came into the kitchen freshly shaved, his hair all tousled.

'To the guildhall.' Thomasina straightened up and turned round. 'Mistress, I would like to pay my respects to Master Blunt.'

Kathryn stared at her nurse's red, podgy face and the determined set of her mouth and chin.

'There's really no need . . .' Colum began.

'Of course you can,' Kathryn said quickly. 'Once I see my patients and they'll be here soon.'

Thomasina thanked her and immediately launched into good-natured banter against the Irishman: how he was an idle wastrel, spending his time mooning over good Christian women. She served Colum oatmeal and placed some bread and butter on the table.

'Shouldn't you go to Kingsmead?' Kathryn asked.

Colum sipped from the spoon and smiled lazily.

'Holbech's there,' he replied, referring to his serjeant-at-arms. 'He'll keep an eye on things. The King will be more concerned by his taxes and Erpingham's death. You found something last night, didn't you, Kathryn?'

Kathryn put her spoon down and went to her chancery office. She brought back the scraps of parchment she'd found at Erpingham's house and smoothed them out on the table between her and Colum.

'This is the Wickerman.' Kathryn pointed to the clumsy drawing of a giant, made out of branches which crisscrossed each other. 'Now the Wickerman, if I remember my father's stories correctly, was a huge figure-shaped cage made out of branches. The ancient people, those who lived here before the Romans came, used to put their prisoners inside the Wickerman, then fire it as an offering to their gods.'

'Yes, yes.' Colum turned the parchment round. 'I have heard similar stories from Ireland.' He glanced at Kathryn. 'And?'

'Well, the drawing represents the tavern, a similar painting of the Wickerman hangs on the sign outside there, more finely depicted, but that doesn't matter. What's important is—' Kathryn pointed to some of the little squares which had been filled with initials. 'What do you see?'

Colum studied them carefully. 'Well, in this square are the letters GP.' He looked quizzically at Kathryn. 'Sir Gervase Percy?'

'Continue,' Kathryn insisted.

'AM.'

'Alan de Murville,' Kathryn replied.

'Of course,' Colum breathed. 'All the guests at the tavern have their initials here.'

'And look at the dates, done in Roman numerals between the Wickerman's legs.'

Colum whistled. 'The sixteenth December.'

'This proves,' Kathryn continued, 'that Erpingham and all those guests arriving at the Wicker Man at the same time was no coincidence.'

Colum tapped the other scraps of parchment. 'And these?'

'Nothing much,' Kathryn said, dabbing at her mouth with a napkin. 'Calculations, sets of figures, though there again the initials appear: GP, AM, even Father Ealdred's.'

'Is it possible,' Colum asked, 'that we wasted our time yesterday? How do we know the guests didn't all plot Erpingham's death? And then each stand as surety for the other?'

'We don't!' Kathryn paused at a knock on the door. 'However, we shall deal with that later, for my patients are arriving.'

They came in a regular stream. The two old spinsters, Eleanor and Maude, complained of sores in their joints and knuckles. Kathryn dispensed some black briony. Bryan the bell-ringer arrived, clutching his belly.

'I have the flux,' he moaned. 'Mistress, it's terrible!'

Kathryn gently felt his podgy stomach, searching for any lump or hardness but found none.

'What have you been eating?'

'Sound bread,' Bryan replied. 'Fresh meat.'

Kathryn smiled at him. 'Then what have you been drinking?'

The bell-ringer blushed. Kathryn told him to be careful about drinking freshly brewed ale and provided a distillation of sweet flag.

'Put that in some good clear water,' Kathryn instructed. 'Let it stand near the fire for at least half an hour, then drink one large spoonful, two or three times a day before you eat. And,' she called out as the bell-ringer, clutching the small phial, sped like an arrow for the door, 'don't drink any ale, at least for a week.'

The last patient was Wynken the watchman. A large, burly, middle-aged man, he staggered into the house, his head twisted slightly to one side. Thomasina, who had more than a soft spot for this stern-faced keeper of the law, fluttered solicitously round him.

'What's the matter?' Kathryn asked.

'I have a spot!' Wynken bellowed. 'A spot on my neck. Can you give me some ointment, Mistress? I'll just rub it on.'

'Sit down,' Kathryn ordered. 'And take off your cloak. Now,' she said firmly as Wynken made to protest, 'how can I treat something I haven't seen?'

The watchman obeyed. Kathryn pulled back the grubby collar of his shirt and grimaced at Thomasina as she glimpsed the angry red swelling that was growing at least an inch from the nape of the watchman's neck.

'That's no spot, Wynken, my lad,' she declared. 'It's what you call a carbuncle.' Kathryn touched it gently and Wynken winced.

'Well, put some cream on it.'

'Aye, I might as well bless it with fairy water,' Kathryn retorted. 'But you want me to treat it?'

'Oh yes, please,' the watchman wailed. 'For the love of God!'

Kathryn paused as she heard another knock on the door. She

smiled and went back to her patient as she heard Luberon's voice from the doorway.

'Now, Wynken,' she said. 'This is going to hurt me more than it's going to hurt you. Thomasina, bring me a candle, two needles and my small cutting knife.'

Alarmed, Wynken made to rise.

'And you can sit still,' Kathryn ordered, pressing him firmly back on the seat.

Thomasina brought the needles and knife, a bowl of hot water and a small roll of bandages. Kathryn made sure the knife and needles were clean and waved them slowly through the flame of the candle. Wynken watched over his shoulder, wincing now and again as his collar caught the boil.

'Oh, Lord, Mistress, what are you doing?'

Kathryn smiled. 'I don't really know but my father, God rest him, always told me that fire is the best cleanser. Now, Wynken, bow your head and say your prayers.'

Kathryn began to talk softly about the weather, then asked why Wynken, an upright widower of the parish, had not yet found another good woman? Kathryn glanced impishly at Thomasina and grinned. As soon as Wynken relaxed, she stopped dabbing at the skin around the angry boil and lanced it neatly, pressing out the pus and cleaning it carefully before applying a small compress made out of dried moss. Wynken yelped. Thomasina told him to shut up but, once Kathryn had finished bandaging, the watchman smiled with relief. He paid his coin and walked out of the door, loudly proclaiming Kathryn's praises.

She washed her hands carefully, put away the phials and bandages and went back into the kitchen where Luberon and Colum were sitting at a table. The Irishman looked worried as he pushed a small canvas bag back into Luberon's hands.

'What's the matter?' Kathryn asked.

'Frenland,' Colum replied. 'Do you remember the fellow who came with me to buy supplies?' He grabbed the bag from Luberon and pushed it across the table.

Kathryn opened it and wrinkled her nose at the sour smell. She pulled out the tattered, bloody remains of a man's coat, then quickly thrust it back in again. 'Frenland's?'

Colum nodded. 'Holbech sent out riders to collect the provisions I had left. The farmstead was not far from the crossroads where Frenland left me. Further along a trackway, well, they found that. According to Master Luberon, it would appear Frenland was attacked by some wild dogs and badly wounded.' He shrugged. 'Perhaps killed.'

'So, who brought it to you, Simon?' Kathryn asked.

The little clerk looked sheepishly down at his hands.

'Frenland's wife came to the guildhall. She was carrying that.' He looked askance at Colum. 'She was making all sorts of allegations against you.'

Colum groaned and cupped his chin in his hand.

'She has a face like vinegar,' Colum murmured. 'And a tongue like a snake. What is she claiming, Simon?'

'That you deserted Frenland, that you panicked or that something else happened . . .' Luberon's voice trailed off.

'Such as?' Kathryn asked sharply.

Luberon squirmed in his seat. 'Well,' he mumbled. 'She said Colum may have even killed him.'

'Nonsense!' Kathryn declared.

Luberon looked at Colum. 'You should go out there, Irishman, and confront her.'

Kathryn grabbed the sack from the table and pushed it into a corner near the hearth.

'No, Colum, you won't! We have business at the guildhall.' She looked sharply at him. 'Something terrible happened in Blunt's house but not the way it was described. Mistress Frenland will just have to wait.'

Kathryn asked Thomasina to get their cloaks and things ready.

'What's he like, this Frenland?' Kathryn continued.

Colum shrugged. 'A good man, easygoing. He served with Lord Hastings in the recent war: his wife's something of a scold but Frenland was good with horses.'

'What did you talk about?' Kathryn asked. 'I mean, as you rode to collect the supplies?'

Colum pulled a face. 'We talked about Canterbury, the stables.' He shuffled his feet in embarrassment.

'What else?' Kathryn demanded.

'Rumours about your husband.' Colum held up his hand. 'For God's sake, Kathryn, there was no harm in that!' He scratched his head. ' "I pray Jesus, to cut short their lives, of those who will not be governed by their wives." ' Colum grinned sheepishly. 'The Wife of Bath's words. Frenland seems to have proved them correct.'

Kathryn shook her head. 'Aye, and doesn't the Wife of Bath end with: "Those old and querulous niggards with their pence. Oh send them soon a mortal pestilence." ' She pointed down at the bag. 'I will deal with Mistress Frenland when we return.'

Behind Kathryn's back Colum winked at Luberon. On reflection, the Irishman was not too upset by Mistress Frenland's accusations. She had no proof for what she alleged and the man had deserted without a by-your-leave. Colum was more intrigued by Kathryn's white-faced anger and air of purpose. Usually she was serene, slightly sardonic, and Colum felt flattered by her brusque refutation of the allegations against him. He and Luberon followed her out into the street. Colum immediately slipped, crashing down onto the icy cobbles.

'By Mogglin's cock!' he cursed and got to his feet, rubbing his arm and knocking the dirty ice from his cloak.

Kathryn came back. 'Colum?'

'Nothing,' he said. 'No harm except to my pride.'

'I meant to tell you,' Luberon confessed, 'the snow may be going but the ice is dangerous.'

Kathryn found the clerk's words prophetic. Ottemelle Lane and all the streets were covered in sheets of ice. However, this hadn't prevented the crowds thronging out to buy supplies in the market where the stalls, booths and shops were doing a thriving business. Nevertheless, time and again, they saw people slip and fall. Thomasina, gingerly following them, had to stop and lean against a house, her sides aching with laughter: Goldere the clerk, in his tight breeches and high-heeled boots, his curly hair prinked and waved, was strutting about only to go crashing down on his bottom, his mouth rounded in an O of stupefaction. Moreover, because of his fanciful footwear, Goldere found it nigh impossible to get to his feet.

The dung carts were also out, trying to remove the mounds of frozen refuse that blocked the way. Two bailiffs from St. Margaret's Street had broken the ice on the sewer down the centre: the stench from the curdled refuse lying there was so strong passersby had to cover their noses and mouths. A pig that had frozen beneath the mound of snow had also been uncovered and beggars, armed with short sticks or cutting knives, were trying to slice portions of meat from its frozen carcase. At the Buttermarket the bailiffs and beadles were filling the stocks with those malefactors who had broken the curfew or committed petty crimes during the great freeze. A pickpocket, caught for the second time, was having his ears nailed to a cross slat of a post. A forger, facing his third indictment, screamed, drowning the cries of the marketplace as the city executioner branded his cheek with a burning iron, a permanent sign of his past dishonesty. A whore, cursing and spitting, had her grimy grey buttocks whipped at the tail of a cart. Two butchers who'd sold putrid meat had to stand on the cross with the meat tied against their nose and mouth. Urchins and beggars, eager for mischief after the loneliness of the last few days, gathered round and pelted these and other malefactors with snowballs and pieces of refuse. Peasants trudged in from the countryside either wheeling hand-barrows or carrying packs lashed to their bowed backs, eager to sell their goods and raise some cash lest the snows return. A song-seller practised a new carol on the steps of a tavern whilst a black-faced traveller stood in his garish rags on the steps of St. Andrew's Church and talked of his travels east of Eden.

Kathryn and her companions walked up the High Street, pausing outside the Chequer of Hope as a funeral cortege wound its way down to St. Helen's Church. The death cart was full of coffins, nothing more than simple pinewood boxes squeezed in and not properly nailed. A passerby told Kathryn how the corpses belonged to an entire family who had been found frozen in their house.

At the guildhall they found merchants, lawyers and city officials thronging the steps eager to exchange news and resume the normal course of events. These stood aside and bowed respectfully as Colum passed. Even though the King's anger against Canterbury for supporting the Lancastrians had now relented, Colum was still known, respected and even feared as the Crown's representative in the city. Inside the guildhall a tipstaff took them along a gallery then down steep steps to the cellars and dungeons. There was no light or heating there, no roaring fire or glowing brazier and Kathryn shivered at the dank cold. She looked over her shoulder at Thomasina. Usually the old nurse commented on everything she saw as they passed, but apart from her merriment at Goldere's fall on the ice, Thomasina had been strangely taciturn and rather secretive.

'You want to see Blunt?' The hooded gaoler came out of the darkness jangling his keys. He bowed respectfully at Colum, yellow-gapped teeth bared in a grin. 'I didn't see you, sir, nor the fine ladies.'

'Just show us Blunt's cell,' Colum snapped.

The gaoler waved them on into the darkness. They followed him down to where a lone sconce torch flickered above a cell door. The gaoler opened this and gestured them into the narrow, foul-smelling dungeon. Kathryn felt the wet rushes underneath and gagged at the fetid stench: rats scampered in the darkness, then Kathryn saw a shape, huddled in one corner, that moved in a rattle of chains. The gaoler brought a candle and fixed it on an iron spike jutting out of the wall.

'I'd best wait outside,' Luberon murmured.

Thomasina leaned against the wall and watched as Kathryn went and crouched before the huddled figure.

'Master Blunt,' she whispered, 'I'm Kathryn Swinbrooke; you asked to see me.'

The prisoner raised his head. Kathryn felt a surge of pity. Blunt was changed beyond recognition: his hair and beard were matted and dirty, his face looked pallid in the flickering candle light, and spots of fever burned high in the sharp-etched cheek bones.

'So, you did come,' the man croaked. He gestured wearily round the cell. 'No comforts here, Mistress Swinbrooke.' Blunt peered into the darkness. 'And who else?'

'Master Murtagh, King's Commissioner in Canterbury.'

'I have heard of you, Irishman.' Blunt's narrow face broke into a smile. 'And if Kathryn Swinbrooke's here, that must be Thomasina, lissome as ever, eh?'

Only a muted sob was the reply.

'Don't cry,' Blunt said softly. He then began to cough, his whole body twisting in convulsions.

Kathryn watched carefully and saw the blood change to spittle on Blunt's lips.

'Colum,' she snapped. 'For pity's sake, ask for some wine!'

'I have brought some,' Thomasina said.

She passed a small wineskin to Kathryn who pushed it into Blunt's hands.

'Drink,' she urged.

Blunt, white-faced with tearful eyes, undid the stopper, then held it up so the wine splashed into his mouth. He began to cough again but managed to control it, then he leant back against the wall.

'You visited Emma and the boy?'

Kathryn nodded. 'Why did you want to see me, Richard? I hardly know you, though I am sad, whilst my father would have been distraught to see you brought so low.'

'I brought it on myself,' Blunt replied, greedily taking a sip from the wineskin. 'I grew old, Mistress Kathryn. I was good at my art. The silver coins and gold pieces began to fill my purse; then I met Alisoun.' Blunt eased his arms as best he could but his wrists and ankles were secured by metal gyves attached by chains to a clasp on the wall.

'And you killed her and those two young men?' Kathryn asked.

Blunt pushed his face closer. Kathryn didn't flinch at the sour smell from his body or the rankness of his breath.

'I have heard of you, Kathryn. Some say you are the city's best physician. I knew you'd be called to view the corpses. I beg you, for pity's sake, let matters stand as they are. If you really want to know the truth, look in the sanctuary of St. Mildred's Church—just go there.' He grabbed her by the wrist and paused for another paroxysm of coughing to pass. When he lifted his head Kathryn glimpsed the bloody spittle on either side of his mouth. 'Please,' he whispered. 'You know the classical tag: *"Quieta non movere."* '

' "Let sleeping dogs lie",' Kathryn replied.

Behind her she could hear Thomasina weeping gently. Blunt raised his head and looked over Kathryn's shoulder.

'Don't cry for me, Thomasina. I have seen the days and felt the sun on my face. I have known the love of a good woman and I have painted miles and miles of walls. Go to the churches of Rochester, Gravesend and Dover. I'll leave my mark when others are long forgotten.'

'Is there anything we can do?' Kathryn asked.

Blunt shook his head. 'Tell Emma and Peter I love them. They are not to come to the trial. I was born alone, I'll die the same way.' Again he grasped Kathryn's wrist. 'But I know you, Mistress Swinbrooke—for the love of God just hold your peace!'

Kathryn rose to her feet. 'Did you know Sir Reginald Erpingham?' She asked.

Now Blunt smiled. 'Aye, a black-hearted, cruel, soulless bastard. I die a happy man knowing Erpingham's met his just deserts. Do you know he wanted me to come to the Wicker Man? Sent me a message that I had accounts to settle.' Blunt cleared his throat and spat onto the black, soggy floor. 'Well, God has settled my account with him, hasn't he? Erpingham was a blackmailer. He was stupid and deserved to die. If I had gone to that tavern, I probably would have killed him as well.'

'Are you saying that those who did go,' Kathryn asked, 'are guilty of his death?'

'One of them is,' Blunt asserted. 'But that's for God to know and you to find out. Years ago Erpingham hunted me, not because I was a poacher, but because I refused to pay his bribes like the rest.'

'But you know nothing of his death?'

Blunt shook his head. 'God save him, I do not.'

'I have brought you something,' Thomasina called out. She

moved out of the shadows and pushed a small linen-covered package into his manacled hands. 'Some bread, cheese and dried meat.'

'Thank you.' Blunt smiled at Kathryn. 'Now leave, please!'

Colum hammered on the door and the gaoler let them out into the ill-lit passageway.

'What was that all about?' Colum whispered.

Kathryn just shook her head. 'Not now, Colum. We must study those paintings in St. Mildred's: I want Blunt to tell me himself.'

'Did you learn anything?' Luberon asked as they left the Guildhall.

Kathryn turned on the steps and faced them both. She tapped Colum on the chest.

'You are the King's Commissioner, Irishman. You, Simon, are the city clerk. Perhaps it's best, at least for the time being, if I keep my thoughts to myself. But I tell you this, Blunt is a dying man.' She stared across at the white-faced Thomasina. 'We know that, don't we?'

Thomasina nodded.

'He's coughing blood, thick and rich,' Kathryn continued. 'His lungs are rotting.'

'Will he die?' Luberon asked, then smiled apologetically. 'I mean, he will not stand trial for weeks: the city Justices will just refer him to the next assize.'

Kathryn pointed down at the High Street where a group of children were pulling along a yule log.

'I am only a physician,' she answered. 'But if Blunt is still alive on Christmas Day I would be very, very surprised. Now, let's take the side streets. I wish to visit St. Mildred's Church.'

After that Kathryn refused to be drawn. They made their way through the afternoon throng, hurrying past the hucksters, pedlars and tinkers who stood on every corner. In St. Mildred's Church, Kathryn, without a by-your-leave, genuflected before the altar, lit the two great beeswax candles that stood on the sanctuary table and walked into the apse, the circular wall behind the altar. Whilst Colum and Luberon stood behind her holding the candles and Thomasina sat watching sadly from the sanctuary chair, Kathryn carefully studied the pictures Blunt had painted over the last twelve months. One was a bestiary that included a phoenix, a pelican, an owl being mobbed by magpies, even a mermaid. The next was of Christ, naked but for a loincloth, displaying his five wounds. Beside this was a scene depicting the signs of the Zodiac. The largest painting was of three kings sumptuously robed, one with a hawk on his wrist, and their encounter with three grisly skeletons. Kathryn admired the brilliant colours and ingenuity of the artist. The paintings spoke to her just as eloquently as any sermon about the spiritual realities, the transient nature of life and the immediacy of death. However, the last painting, the one Blunt had been working on the very day he had gone home for his mortal confrontation with Alisoun, caught her attention. A scene from the Old Testament, Abraham offering his son Isaac to God. The boy was strapped to the altar and Abraham stood staring up at the angel who was trying to restrain him, gripping his hand with the dagger clenched there.

'Bring the candles closer,' she urged.

Colum and Luberon obeyed. Kathryn studied the scene again. She recalled the face in that ghastly cell at the guildhall and stared at the figure of Abraham. She then examined the patriarch's hand and noticed how the dagger was pointed inwards to his own chest rather than down at his son. Kathryn touched it carefully and smiled bleakly at Colum.

'I have seen enough,' she whispered. 'I know the truth.'

Chapter 8

As Kathryn and Colum walked back through the gathering dusk, Vavasour, the tax collector's clerk, stood staring out of his chamber window. Kathryn would have hardly recognised the nervous little clerk: no more twitching or irritable gestures, Vavasour stood stock still, his face impassive, eyes unblinking, as he glared into the darkness. Now and again he would rub his eyes or smile secretively as if savouring some private joke.

'Everything comes to those who wait,' Vavasour whispered to himself. He dug his thumbs into the broad leather belt round his meagre waist. Erpingham was gone, not beforetime, Vavasour concluded. No more would he sit, the poor man at Erpingham's beck and call, like some favourite mongrel being tossed the odd cut of meat or stale biscuit. Vavasour chewed his lip. 'If the meat's gone,' he murmured, 'the gravy still remains.'

To be sure, Vavasour reflected, that sharp-eyed bitch Swinbrooke had discovered the secret house in St. Alphage's Lane, but Erpingham had other hidden caches across the shire. In time, Vavasour intended to help himself to all of these. Oh, he'd miss Erpingham! The wicked bastard used to regale Vavasour with his sexual exploits: how some high-stepping widow had pleasured him in bed rather than pay her full dues. Erpingham, with money salted away with the bankers, had a veritable fortune to pay for his illicit pursuits. Vavasour recalled the night Erpingham had the nightmare. The tax collector had always boasted about his evil ancestor and his connection with that particular chamber at the Wicker Man: now Erpingham had paid for the folly of staying in a tavern surrounded by his enemies. He had been murdered so mysteriously, yet—and Vavasour rubbed his hands in glee—he could prove how it was done.

'Many a slip 'twixt cup and lip,' Vavasour whispered and soon he would prove his point.

The little clerk stared at the hour candle burning quietly on the table. The flame had already reached the seventeenth red circle: five o'clock in the evening, that was the time the message had given. At five o'clock Vavasour was to cross the Great Meadow opposite the tavern. He was to faithfully follow the footsteps through the snow, down the hill to the dell on the edge of the meadow. There, Vavasour would receive his share of the hundreds of pounds stolen from the tax collector's saddlebags.

The clerk sat on the edge of his bed and pulled his boots up his spindly legs.

'Why such a desolate spot?' he grumbled.

However, he had put on his sword belt with a sword and dagger pushed through its rings, and he also picked up the small arbalest and stuck five of the quarrels into his belt. Vavasour was no fool: he would go armed and there would be a lantern burning. Vavasour swung his cloak about him, concealing the arbalest beneath it and left his chamber.

'Are you going out?' a servant asked as he came downstairs.

'Just for a short walk.' Vavasour grinned enigmatically.

'It's cold and wintry,' Tobias Smithler said from where he stood at the wine tuns filling a jug.

Vavasour stared round the taproom. Only the old knight Sir Gervase Percy was there, sitting at the corner of the hearth toasting his toes before the fire; he looked up, narrow-eyed, at Vavasour.

'Don't go far,' he warned. 'You heard the Irishman. We are all to stay here until this business is finished.'

Vavasour forced a smile.

'What about Sir Reginald's body?' the landlord asked.

'Well, it's now in the death house at the castle,' Vavasour replied, his hand on the latch. 'His soul's gone to God and his body is going to rot. What more can I do?'

He stepped through the door, slamming it behind him and crossed the frozen cobbled yard. At the end of the trackway he paused. A mist was seeping in, thick and white, shrouding the road and trees on either side. Vavasour went across, then jumped as a figure loomed out of the darkness.

'What the . . . ?' Vavasour's hand tightened on the crossbow.

'It's only me, sir.'

Vavasour relaxed as he recognised Raston, an old servant from the tavern. The man looked guilty and kept his hand beneath his serge cloak.

Poaching, Vavasour thought—so that's where Master and Mistress Smithler obtain their fresh meat. Vavasour crossed the trackway; as Sir Reginald would say, he'd remember that. Such information was worth the price of a free meal—or, then again, a love tryst with Mistress Smithler? Vavasour felt the excitement stir in his loins. She was toothsome enough, or so his master said: a rather languid beauty with her blond hair falling about her face. Vavasour wondered whether she'd share her favours if he offered enough. Reginald always claimed she would.

'If you offer enough,' the tax collector would trumpet when in his cups, 'any wench will happily oblige.'

Vavasour opened the gate and entered the meadow. Well, soon he would have enough gold and silver to satisfy all his desires. Now he concentrated on trudging through the knee-deep snow. He faithfully followed the footsteps of the person who had gone before him. Vavasour paused. Was there something wrong? Why meet out in the dell of the Great Meadow? Vavasour's mouth tightened. Well, he'd keep his side of the bargain. He would climb to the brow of the hill and, if he saw no lantern winking below him, then he would trudge back to the tavern. He'd have a good meal and go straight into Canterbury, seek out the Irishman and turn King's evidence. The clerk paused. Should he do that? Somewhere in the darkness an angry vixen yipped hungrily at the full moon and an owl, hunting fruitlessly along the hedgerows, hooted mournfully.

I am like that, Vavasour thought: a hunter, but either way, I will not leave empty-handed. He trudged on; his boots were good, the finest leather, but the snow was deep. Now and again Vavasour shivered at the icy white wetness against his thighs. He would have liked to turn back. He heard a sound behind him and paused, turning round so quickly he nearly stumbled and fell. Was someone following him?

'Is anyone there?'

But all he could glimpse was a sea of whiteness and the faint lights of the tavern. At last Vavasour reached the top of the hill. He brushed the snow from his cloak and looked down into the dell. Under the moonlight the field shimmered like silver. His eyes searched the darkness, trying to peer through the shifting mist; then he saw it, the lantern glowing eerily, beckoning him on. Vavasour made his decision. Chuckling softly to himself, he went down the hill, following the furrows in the snow, heading directly for the lantern light. Its glow grew stronger, drawing him on. Vavasour now comforted himself: he could see the sense of meeting out in the open, well away from prying eyes and inquisitive looks. He just wished it was all over. How much had Sir Reginald collected? Hundreds of pounds! A veritable fortune! Vavasour could change his name, perhaps buy a manor on the Welsh march! Or amongst the soft green fields of Devon and become a lord of the soil! Vavasour paused when he reached the foot of the hill. He stared across at the lantern light.

'I am coming!' he called. 'Is everything all right? I didn't know how you could meet me here.' Vavasour narrowed his eyes, he couldn't position the height or exact position of the lantern. He sighed and trudged on. 'I want more than half!' he called. 'Perhaps two thirds?' Suddenly he paused, his heart skipping a beat. Beneath him the ground began to crack. 'Oh, Lord!' Vavasour ran on but the ice underfoot gave way and he plunged waist-deep into the frozen water.

'Help me!'

The lantern seemed to be moving.

'Oh, Christ, help me!'

Weighted down by his sword belt and arbalest, Vavasour sank beneath the icy water, his body engulfed in one tongue of pain. He flailed about, but his cloak was too heavy. His head felt as if it had been dragged back. The cold was excruciating. He made one last lunge but the water dragged him down. Vavasour's eyes closed as he slipped quickly into unconsciousness.

Above him the young hunting owl, disturbed by the strange sounds from below, hooted once more before flying into the dark sanctuary of the trees.

Kathryn rose early the next morning. For a while she played with Wuf out in the garden. The lad had fashioned himself a game, little wooden posts set on the icy carp pond which he would try and knock down with the polished wooden disc he had carved. Kathryn was pleased to see the thaw continue: the sky was blue and the sun surprisingly strong. She stared round the garden.

'The herb gardens will be well watered,' she remarked, tousling Wuf's hair. 'In spring there will be a good harvest. Plenty of work here, Wuf, plucking and drying.'

'I'll be good at that,' the little boy said.

'Of course you will,' Thomasina called from the kitchen doorway. 'But, come in, both of you, its time to break your fast.'

Kathryn pulled a face at Wuf. 'We'd best obey.'

They went in and sat round the table, Agnes joining them, for a bowl of oatmeal spiced with nutmeg and covered in hot milk. After this Thomasina served a platter of small manchet loaves, a little jug of butter and some jam made of juicy blackberries from the store of preserves Thomasina had prepared earlier in the year. Agnes, however, sat pale-faced and silent, refusing to be drawn by Wuf's teasing.

'What is the matter, girl?' Thomasina asked.

The young maid lifted her face, her light blue eyes brimming with tears. 'It's Wormhair,' she declared, referring to the love of her life.

Wormhair served as a clothmaker's apprentice during the week and, every Sunday, was the clumsiest altar boy at St. Mildred's Church.

Kathryn's heart skipped a beat at what might be wrong: Agnes was a surrogate daughter or younger sister. A foundling brought home by Kathryn's father, Agnes had always insisted on working and would sulk for days if Kathryn tried to stop her. Sensible and level-headed, Agnes, however, had an undying passion for Wormhair. Despite his cheeky face and greasy hair which always stood up in great tufts or spikes, Agnes regarded Wormhair as her Sir Galahad.

'Is he well?' Kathryn asked.

'Well no, he's . . .' Agnes licked her lips. 'Whilst you were out last night, Mistress, Wormhair came round, suffering pains and spasms in his belly. I know there are no patients coming this morning so—'

'Mistress Kathryn never dispenses medicines on Saturdays,' Thomasina trumpeted.

'But I told him to come,' Agnes continued in a rush; then her mouth fell open at the sudden rapping on the door. 'And I think that's him.'

But it was Luberon who came striding into the kitchen, blithely shaking the drifting snow off his cloak, ignoring Thomasina's shrieks of horror.

'There has been another death at the Wicker Man,' he announced grandly. 'Vavasour, the stupid fool, went walking across the Great Meadow. He went down the hill and, for God knows what reason, tried to cross the small mere or pond at the bottom.' Luberon sat down and smiled knowingly at Thomasina. 'And a bowl of your oatmeal for me, oh fairest of the fair.'

Thomasina, who had a secret liking for this rubicund-faced clerk, brought a heated bowl from the hearth, pushing the jug of milk and pots of honey and nutmeg towards him.

'Why on earth would he do that?' Colum came into the kitchen, holding the stirrup he had been mending.

Luberon cleared his mouth. 'I said death, but, then again, it could be murder. Old Raston, one of the servants and probably a poacher, saw Vavasour cross the trackway. Raston went into the tavern and reported what he had seen to the Smithlers, who also seemed nonplussed. Anyway, his curiosity aroused, Raston decided to follow Vavasour. He got to the top of the hill; through the mist he saw Vavasour pause at the edge of the mere, then he began to walk across. Now, this is where it turns strange. Raston is certain someone holding a lantern was waiting for Vavasour.'

'A lantern!' Colum exclaimed.

'Well, yes, that's how Raston could see what was going on.' Luberon sprinkled nutmeg over the oatmeal. 'And then it happened. Raston heard the ice snap. He saw Vavasour floundering around but he was too old and the mere too far away to be of any help. Raston ran down the hill but, by the time he reached the edge of the mere, Vavasour was gone and so had the light.'

Luberon glanced across at Kathryn. 'That's all I know. The boy the Smithlers sent to me reported how his master would try to drag the mere for Vavasour's body.' Luberon smiled thinly. 'But they are already talking about ghosts: how the curse of the Wicker Man lured Vavasour to his death.' The clerk breathed noisily out. 'We will have to go back there.'

'We were going anyway,' Kathryn declared. 'I have certain questions to ask all those guests.' She shook her head at Luberon's enquiring look. 'No, not now, Simon.' Kathryn rose and went to the corner of the hearth where the sack containing the remains of Frenland's cloak lay. 'I want to ask you a favour, Simon.' She winked quickly at Colum. She went and collected her father's greasy vellum map of Kent from her writing office and handed it to Luberon. 'The roads are passable now,' she said. 'No man knows Kent and its byways like you, Simon. I want you to have a word with Colum and go back to the crossroads where Frenland disappeared. Colum will tell you the exact path he took. Kathryn smiled at Luberon. 'Please make enquiries at the farmsteads and villages along that trackway. They may know something about Frenland's death.'

'But I was going to . . .' Colum caught Kathryn's warning look.

'Master Murtagh,' she said in mock solemnity. 'You are the King's Commissioner in Canterbury. The Crown's tax collector has been murdered and, perhaps, the same fate has befallen his clerk. Your duty is to go to the Wicker Man.'

Luberon, a master of the law and its procedures, nodded wisely. Kathryn leaned across the table and grasped his podgy hand.

'Simon, please do this for me and so help clear Colum of these malicious rumours.'

'I'll need an escort,' the little clerk declared.

'Colum will provide one,' Kathryn replied. 'He'll write a letter to Holbech for you.'

'But I also need to question you about Blunt,' Luberon added.

'On your return,' Kathryn promised. She gestured at Colum. 'Don't be such a slug-a-bed, Irishman. Oh, for goodness' sake!'

Kathryn swept back to her chancery. She seized a piece of parchment, quill and ink horn and wrote out the authorisation for Luberon to take to Kingsmead. She then called Colum, melted a little red wax upon which she impressed the seal of his signet ring. Colum, tongue between lips, laboriously signed the letter.

'Why all the hurry, woman?' he asked half crossly.

Kathryn stood on tiptoe and kissed him on each cheek.

'Don't "woman" me, Irishman. Just do what you are told. Master Luberon will go to Kingsmead and show this letter to Holbech. He has got my father's map, which he'd better not lose, then he can search for the truth behind this Frenland business.'

Colum stared at her. 'If I called you woman, would you kiss me again?'

Kathryn slapped him playfully on the wrist. 'I want Luberon out of here,' she said. 'I don't want to be questioned about the murders at the Blunt household.'

'Why?'

'In a while,' Kathryn replied, 'I'll tell you.'

'But why send him on a wild goose chase?'

'Oh, it's no fool's errand,' Kathryn replied. 'As soon as I rose this morning, I studied Master Frenland's cloak again. I was rather intrigued: I discovered small fragments of leather.'

Colum frowned down at her.

'Just think about it.' Kathryn grinned. 'I don't want to raise expectations, but, for God's sake, Colum, much as I like him, send Master Luberon about his business.'

Colum strode back into the kitchen. Kathryn heard his effusive flattery, telling Luberon that, in this matter, the clerk was his most faithful and able lieutenant.

'Easy with the flattery, Irishman,' Kathryn whispered. 'Thomasina!'

The old nurse came waddling in, the sleeves of her smock pushed back above her elbow, her hands and thick wrists covered in flour.

'Thomasina, you know that Blunt's dying.'

'Aye, that cough!'

'Aye, the cough,' Kathryn repeated. 'Now, please stay here and look after Agnes and Wuf. However, if you have the opportunity, find out who was Blunt's physician. Go and ask him questions, tell him you are acting for me.' Kathryn stared down at her fingers. 'But, Thomasina, do not tell anyone about what you learn.'

Kathryn and Colum left a few minutes later, hurrying down Wistraet into the parish of St. Mary of the Castle, then along an alleyway to the Wicker Man. Kathryn refused to answer any of Colum's questions, but she told him to watch his step because she had the King's business to do and not the King's Commissioner to look after, should he sprain his wrist or graze his arm. They arrived in the taproom just after Tobias Smithler and a number of servants brought in Vavasour's water-soaked corpse.

'Another death, Mistress Swinbrooke,' the landlord called out. 'The corpse, where shall we put it?'

Kathryn pointed to a table. Smithler was about to object.

'For God's sake, man!' Colum ordered. 'It won't be for long.'

Smithler nodded at the servitors who laid Vavasour out along the trestle table. Kathryn had seen many corpses but this one was ghastly. Vavasour was both drowned and frozen. His wispy hair stood up like icicles whilst the skin of his face had turned a whiteish-blue, freezing into a mask, the awful rictus of his death agony. Kathryn quickly and expertly searched the corpse.

'What are you looking for?' Sir Gervase bellowed.

'I am looking for a wound,' Kathryn replied. She indicated to Colum to turn the corpse over. 'But I can't find any: this man drowned.'

'An accident?' Smithler asked.

Kathryn stared down at the hideous face. 'What on earth was Vavasour doing walking on a frozen mere?'

The anxious-faced de Murvilles just shook their heads.

'I can understand any of you going out for a breath of fresh air, but why cross the Great Meadow on such a night in the middle of winter? And why walk through almost a foot of snow to cross a frozen mere?'

'He wouldn't know it was there.' Raston, the gnarl-faced poacher, pushed his way to the front of the group. 'He was lured to his death, Mistress! I saw the lantern winking in the darkness. Vavasour was heading for that. I heard him call out as if greeting someone. Then he began to walk across the mere. The rest you know.'

'Let's visit it,' Colum declared, clapping the old poacher on the shoulder. 'And I should be most grateful if you, Master Raston, would come with us and tell us exactly what you saw.' Colum glanced at the guests. 'The rest of you are welcome to come; however, if what Master Raston says is the truth, then we are dealing with no accident but bloody-handed murder. Have any of you searched Vavasour's room?'

'No.' Smithler shook his head. 'I wouldn't let anyone go near it until Master Luberon came. By the way, where is he?'

'Involved in other business,' Kathryn remarked. 'But come, let's visit the Great Meadow.'

Her words had the same effect as a hanging judge's death sentence. The servants began whispering amongst themselves. The guests, the de Murvilles, Father Ealdred and even the hard-bitten serjeant Standon glared despairingly at one another.

'Master Standon,' Kathryn called out. 'I would be grateful if you stayed and put a guard on Erpingham's and Vavasour's chambers.'

117

'There's little point in any of that,' Blanche Smithler said. 'Sir Reginald's room has been cleaned.' She pointed at Vavasour's purse. 'And each chamber only has one key.'

Kathryn opened the slime-covered wallet. Inside were a few coins and a long, rusting iron key. She handed the coins to the landlord.

'You'd best keep these,' she said. 'And, for the moment, if you don't mind, I'll keep the key.'

Led by Raston they all trooped out of the tavern, across the trackway and into the Great Meadow. The path through the snow was fairly easy because of those who had beaten a track down to the mere to recover Vavasour's corpse. Nevertheless, Kathryn carefully studied the snow on either side of this manmade path.

'You are looking for other footsteps?' Colum whispered, coming up beside her. He stopped and narrowed his eyes, shielding them with his hand against the glare of the sun. 'I can't see anything,' he murmured. 'Some bird's marks.' He pointed to his right. 'And some fox prints but nothing else.'

They climbed the small hill, paused on the brow and stared down at the mere. In the daylight Kathryn could see it must be one of those small but quite treacherous pools or ponds which, in winter, made this countryside so dangerous to cross. It lay at the foot of the hill, three sides of it nothing but clear meadow. On the far side a high bank or vallum rose steeply to another hillock.

'I can't understand it,' Kathryn murmured as they walked down towards the mere. 'Raston said he saw someone else on that mere with a lantern but I can't see how that was possible.'

'The murderer could have walked back in Vavasour's footsteps.'

'Impossible,' Kathryn replied. 'Raston saw the light and Vavasour walking on the mere but then both the clerk and the light disappeared, which leaves two conclusions. First, the person Vavasour was meeting also drowned when the ice broke. Or, secondly, he or she left the mere by another route. In which case there should be some sign of this.'

They reached the edge of the mere. Kathryn gazed across at

the black, icy water and recalled her father's warning about such places. She looked over her shoulder at Smithler.

'How deep would you say this was?'

The landlord blew his lips out. 'Ten, twelve feet, Mistress.'

Kathryn gazed on either side. 'And the width?'

'About sixty yards.'

'Raston,' she asked. 'Are you certain about what you saw last night?'

'Before God and his angels, Mistress, I saw the lantern.' Raston pointed across the mere's shimmering black water. 'There was a mist which made the light look eerie but it was definitely a lantern.'

'What do you mean by eerie?' Colum asked.

'Well, it was like seeing a light out at sea. Or the sun through thick cloud. I glimpsed a glow of fire and a ring of gold around it. It must have been quite a heavy lantern.'

'And it was on the mere?' Kathryn insisted. 'Not to the side or at the top of the vallum?'

The old poacher shook his head. 'No, Mistress, and I hadn't drunk a drop of ale. Vavasour must have been within a few yards of the lantern when the ice broke and in he went.' Raston scratched his unshaven cheek. 'He shrieked like a rabbit in a noose.'

Colum began to walk round the edge of the mere, then turned to stare back at the group. All the guests had accompanied them, even the elegant Lady de Murville, but apart from Kathryn, the only person he could trust was Raston.

Colum pointed at him. 'You walk round that side of the mere whilst I walk around here.'

'What are we looking for?' Raston called.

'Footprints, any sign of someone else crossing the mere from a different point. Mistress Kathryn is standing where Vavasour probably did?'

The old servant nodded.

'And you, Master Smithler, when you fished poor Vavasour out?'

'We stood here,' the landlord replied. 'We used rods and ropes with hooks on the end. It was easy enough. Vavasour was floating just beneath the surface.'

'Did you find anything else, the lantern or some trace of who was holding it?'

'No.' Smithler shook his head. 'The lantern would have sunk and be lost in the slime and mud at the bottom.'

Colum nodded and snapped his fingers for Raston to continue walking. Kathryn watched both of them go. The Great Meadow fell silent except for the raucous cawing of the crows from a small copse a little distance away. At last both Colum and Raston reached the vallum that which bordered the Great Meadow.

'Have you seen anything?' Colum called across.

Raston shook his head. 'Nothing at all, sir! Pure as driven snow. Some fox prints, a hare, perhaps a badger.'

'Anything?' Colum repeated.

Again the old servant shook his head and trooped carefully back to join Kathryn and the rest of the guests. Colum climbed onto the bank of the snow-covered vallum, going as closely as possible to the edge of the mere. He then walked slowly back, shaking his head.

'Nothing,' he said. 'No sign of anyone along the edge of the mere or on the vallum.' Colum pulled a face. 'I have never seen the like of this,' he said. 'Oh, I have heard the stories about will-o'-the-wisps or scouts deliberately misleading the enemy across marshy land during a mist but this is a mystery. Someone walked onto that mere, leaving no trace of how they got there or how they left, and lured Vavasour to his death.'

'And, before you ask again,' Raston broke in, 'I saw that lantern. I saw Vavasour drown. I did not see anyone else go on to the mere.'

Kathryn glanced at the landlord and his guests.

'When Vavasour left, where were you all?'

'I was in the taproom,' Sir Gervase said. 'And so was the landlord and his wife.'

'And you, Father Ealdred?'

'He was with us,' Alan de Murville said. 'He can vouch for us

120

and we can vouch for him. We heard Vavasour leave and wondered why he was going out on such a cold night.'

'And Standon?'

'He was in the stables,' Raston replied. 'Playing dice with his soldiers. They were supposed to be tending the horses.'

'You met Vavasour going out?' Kathryn asked.

'Oh yes,' the old servant asserted. 'I had been along the trackway looking for fresh meat.'

'You didn't come from the meadow?' Kathryn asked.

The old man laughed harshly. 'In winter you don't catch rabbits in a snow-filled meadow, Mistress. I went into a copse and set my snares amongst the bushes.'

'Must we stay here any longer?' Lady Margaret de Murville spoke up quickly. 'Mistress Swinbrooke, my feet are like blocks of ice.' She gazed around the snow-filled meadow. 'I never believed in ghosts. Or the vengeance of God taking such a practical form.' The noblewoman shivered and pulled at her ermine-lined cloak. 'But now I do.' She turned and went back up the hill.

The rest made to follow. Colum looped his arm through Kathryn's.

'What do you think?' he asked.

'I don't think anything, Colum. Old Raston is definitely telling the truth. Why would Vavasour cross such an icy expanse in the dark unless he was meeting someone involved in Sir Reginald's death?'

'Or Vavasour's own accomplice?'

'Perhaps,' Kathryn replied. 'Whatever, Vavasour was definitely lured to his death.' She smoothed the hair from her face and rubbed some warmth into her cheeks. 'But who murdered him is a mystery: no one left that tavern and no one came back.'

'What about Raston?' Colum asked.

'No.' Kathryn shook her head. 'He's too open, too sincere. He need not have told us what he saw. We face two problems, Colum, or should I say three? Why did Vavasour leave? Whom did he hope to meet? And how did that person lure him onto the mere?'

'Someone who knew the area well?'

Raston, trudging in front of them, looked back over his shoulder.

'Is everything all right?' he asked.

The rest of the guests stopped as they reached the brow of the hill.

'How many of you knew about the mere?' Kathryn asked.

A chorus of assent greeted her words.

'I suppose we all did,' Alan de Murville added. 'In summertime it's a pleasant place to walk, though apparently Vavasour forgot about the mere.'

Kathryn smiled her thanks and they all trudged on.

'Lady Murville may be right,' Kathryn commented. 'Perhaps it was some hideous ghost!'

Chapter 9

Kathryn, Colum and the guests removed their cloaks and dried themselves off in front of the roaring taproom fire. Once again Blanche Smithler, her irate husband beside her, served light refreshments, cups of warm posset and a platter of doucettes.

'You may dismiss the servants,' Kathryn declared. 'What I have to say is not for their ears.'

'All this is costing me money,' Smithler moaned.

'Shut up!' Colum snapped. 'The thaw will continue and the King intends to be at Westminster for crown-wearing during the Christmas festivities. A report of all this will be despatched to him and, believe me, Master Smithler, if this matter is not satisfactorily resolved, the King will send others.' He walked towards the landlord who was wiping his hands nervously on his apron. 'Have you met His Majesty's henchman? The puissant, though rather choleric Richard, Duke of Gloucester?'

'The King's brother?' Smithler asked.

'Yes, the King's brother. He will come here with his soldiers. And, I assure you, Gloucester is none too subtle in defending his brother's prerogative. So, all of you, listen and, on your loyalty, speak the truth.'

'What's this about?' Sir Gervase piped up, half rising from his chair as Smithler beat a hasty retreat.

'It's about lies,' Kathryn retorted. 'You, Sir Gervase, Lord and Lady de Murville, Father Ealdred. You all told us lies. You claimed to have come to the Wicker Man because you were travelling hither and thither.'

The guests stared guiltily back. Lady de Murville's face became ashen.

'You came here,' Kathryn continued, 'because Erpingham summoned you here, didn't he?' She drew from her wallet the pieces of paper she had found in Erpingham's house in St. Alphage's Lane. 'Here is a drawing of a wickerman; in the branches are certain initials, all of yours, alongside a date, the beginning of this week. On these other scraps of parchment are mysterious calculations against each of your names.' Kathryn arranged her cloak over the back of her chair. 'Now, either you answer my questions or Master Murtagh will issue you each with a subpoena to answer before Star Chamber at Westminster.'

'It's not . . .' Father Ealdred began, but he lapsed into silence as Sir Gervase sprang to his feet.

'Let us tell the truth,' the old knight declared. 'We have done wrong, Mistress Swinbrooke.' Sir Gervase went to warm his hands before the fire. 'Sir Reginald was an evil man and he was a blackmailer. The harvest had not been good, and the civil war between York and Lancaster wreaked terrible damage. Now the King is back in his own and men like Erpingham tour the shires collecting royal dues: arrears of taxes or the reassessment of property.' He paused as Standon came downstairs and pulled up a stool to sit beside Father Ealdred. 'Ask Standon here. Erpingham was the most ruthless of royal agents. He played his little games and I was one of his victims. He arrived on my estates and asked to see my bailiff. A tax assessment was to be made but Erpingham seemed as benevolent as some good-hearted friar.'

Sir Gervase paused and leaned one hand against the hearth piece. He looked older now and, despite the fire, his face had turned a cold grey. 'Let us assume you were worth forty pounds a year,' he went on. 'Erpingham would say "No, let's call it thirty." '

'And the assessment would be made at thirty pounds?' Kathryn asked.

'Of course. Erpingham would leave and everyone would be delighted.'

Sir Gervase pursed his thin lips. 'But then the bastard would return. He was clever with figures. He would claim that, on his first visit, we had not given honest answers but, for a certain amount of silver, he would overlook this and accept the first assessment.'

'Surely,' Colum interrupted, 'you could have appealed to the Sheriff or to the King's Council in London?'

Gervase laughed sourly. 'And say what? That the tax collector had given us an assessment which was too low and he was now blackmailing us?' He shook his head. 'What proof would we have of that? Erpingham always made sure there were no witnesses about and, as you know, he would claim he only wrote down what he was told.'

Father Ealdred spoke up. 'Can't you see the sheer simplicity of Erpingham's evil? If we protested, that evil man would accuse us of misleading him on the first occasion and, when he came back to make a second, more thorough investigation, we objected.'

'He was like a spider,' de Murville said. 'Once you were caught in his web there was no way out. You became party to his game and he was its master.' Lord Alan spread his hands. 'We were caught between a rock and a hard place. If we protested, the Exchequer barons in London would make a thorough reassessment. If we kept quiet, our taxes were low but we had to bribe Erpingham.'

Kathryn glanced across at Colum. He blew his cheeks out, then brushed some crumbs from his lap.

'It's true,' the Irishman declared. 'Each tax collector is expected to make a little profit, usually a percentage of what he obtains. The Crown turns a blind eye to this, overlooking a small evil, as the lawyers say, to achieve a greater good. According to what Sir Gervase and others say, Erpingham had the best of both worlds. He would blackmail those he collected from, and make up any shortfall by being even more grasping.'

'It was worse than that,' Father Ealdred interrupted. 'Erpingham was a born lecher: I think he truly hated women. Sometimes the blackmail would take the form of money or'—his voice faltered—'services rendered.' He played with a tassel of his gown. 'What could we do?' he whispered. 'Master Murtagh, you are a royal official. How could some poor widow woman act? Admit she'd lain all night with Sir Reginald? Or Sir Gervase, could he confess to being party to theft but was now objecting because he was being blackmailed?' The priest laughed abruptly. 'And can you just imagine Sir Reginald before the King's Council in Star Chamber with that whining little varlet Vavasour beside him? He would prove how hard he worked for the Crown: how much silver he'd collected for the Exchequer and now, because of his just labours, he was being cruelly maligned.'

'He beguiled us,' Alan de Murville said. 'We fell into the trap Father Ealdred has described.' He glanced away, embarrassed, and grasped his wife's hand. She raised the other to conceal her face.

'What do you mean?' Kathryn asked.

'He began to make suggestions,' Lord Alan declared defiantly. 'About Lady Margaret. About a night of passion.' The young lord stopped to control his breathing. 'I could have killed him!' he rasped hoarsely. 'Standing in my hall with that piece of dog shit beside him, looking so humble yet enjoying every second of our humiliation.'

'So, why did you come here?' Kathryn asked.

'Oh, Sir Reginald liked his games,' Sir Gervase said, sitting down. 'He would call it his "accounting period". Mistress Swinbrooke, we came here to pay our dues and we had little choice but to dance to Erpingham's tune.' He glanced sideways at the de Murvilles. 'Perhaps he had other plans as well. Anyway, we'd all gathered here. No one dared mention anything: a day and a night, we'd hand our silver over and go our separate ways. Erpingham collected his bribes, well away from prying eyes and not during his official tour of duty.' The old knight sneered. 'A clever, legal defence if anything ever did go wrong. Only this time it did, the snow came. We became prisoners and Erpingham was murdered.'

Colum looked at the royal serjeant. 'Were you party to any of this?'

The soldier scratched his frightened face. 'I, I . . .' He stammered. 'I have told you my thoughts on Sir Reginald. True, I found it strange that people from whom he collected taxes came to this tavern but my task was to protect Sir Reginald and, more importantly, the taxes he carried. I could see nothing wrong . . .'

'Don't lie!' Father Ealdred snarled.

Standon's hand fell to his knife hilt.

'What's this?' Colum came between them. Standon glared hot-eyed over the Irishman's shoulder at Father Ealdred.

'Come on, man,' Colum urged. 'What is the priest alleging?'

'That Erpingham,' Standon grated, 'used to collect taxes from my mother. It was Vavasour's little joke, there was no truth to it. But'—he shot a hand out—'our priest knows all about poisons. I saw him examining Erpingham's corpse and whisper, "Too much, too much was used." '

'Is that true, Father?' Kathryn asked.

'Yes.' Ealdred sighed noisily. 'For my sins, I know a little about physic and the use of herbs: Erpingham's corpse turned so blotchy I knew he must have drunk a great deal of the poison.'

Kathryn nodded, then whispered in Colum's ear before turning to the landlord.

'I should be grateful, sir, if you could arrange for Erpingham's chamber to be opened. Would you take Master Murtagh there? You'll need a hammer, chisel and other tools.'

'Whatever for?' the landlord asked.

'We have found the reason,' Kathryn replied, 'for Erpingham being here. We understand the real hatred between these good people and their wicked tax collector, but the mystery of his murder still remains. To put it bluntly, sir, I want that room properly searched. Master Murtagh will do it.' She handed Colum the key taken from Vavasour's purse. 'And have the dead clerk's chamber searched as well.' She stared around. 'Oh, by the way, where is his corpse?'

'Whilst we were gone,' Smithler replied, 'the servants took it to an outhouse. This is a taproom, Mistress Swinbrooke—the corpse stank!'

Colum, with Smithler trailing behind him, went up the stairs to the first gallery.

'Master Standon,' Kathryn asked. 'Perhaps you will be so good as to assist Master Murtagh.'

The serjeant scurried away, clearly relieved to be free of the tension and anxiety of his companions. Kathryn waited until he was out of the room.

'Do you realise,' she began softly, 'that what you have told me could mean a bill of indictment being laid against each and all of you for the murder of Sir Reginald and his clerk Vavasour, not to mention theft of the royal taxes?' She gestured with her hand at Sir Gervase to keep silent. 'You had both the motive and the means. And you certainly stood to profit. Can you imagine what the royal Justices might find if they began to search and dug really deep?' She pointed at the pale-faced Ealdred. 'You mentioned a widow woman in your village, Father, whom Sir Reginald abused. What is your relationship with that woman?'

The priest stared stonily back.

'And you, Sir Gervase, a clever lawyer might insinuate that you were not Sir Reginald's victim but really his accomplice.' She glanced at the de Murvilles. 'Indeed, the same could be said for all of you.' Kathryn saw the worried look in Blanche Smithler's face. 'Nor do you escape free,' Kathryn continued relentlessly. 'Sir Reginald chose this tavern. The Justices will ask if you and your husband were his accomplices.'

'But it is not true!' Lady Margaret sat forward in her chair, her hands gripped tightly in her lap, her face drawn and white. 'Erpingham was a viper, a malignant creature.'

'So you hated him?' Kathryn asked.

Lady Margaret's eyes blazed with fury.

'I despised him!' she spat. 'I hated him! And, I'll be honest, I'm glad he's dead!'

'If you said as much before King's Bench,' Kathryn retorted, 'Your high birth would not save you. Now, one of you did kill Sir Reginald Erpingham.'

Kathryn paused at the banging and crashing that broke out above her, followed by silence, then shouts of surprise. Standon came running down the stairs.

'Mistress Swinbrooke, Mistress Swinbrooke,' he gasped. 'Come quickly!'

'What is it?'

'We lifted the floorboards just beneath Erpingham's bed. We found—well, you'd best come and see.'

Kathryn, followed by the rest, made her way upstairs along the gallery. The door to Erpingham's chamber had been rehung but inside all was chaos. Floorboards had been hauled up and the dust, hanging thick in the air, made her cough. Where the bed had been, Colum now sat, squatting above a gap, floorboards piled to one side.

'Open a window!' he ordered Standon.

The serjeant hurried to obey.

'Come, physician!' Colum gently mocked.

Kathryn went and stared down at the human skull and bones that lay in the dust beneath the floorboards.

'God in his heaven!'

Kathryn knelt down beside Colum and pulled out the skull and bones, all gray-white with age.

'Another murder victim?' Colum asked.

'Too old,' Kathryn replied, studying the skull: the lower jaw was missing and the teeth nothing more than dark stumps. She turned the skull over and carefully examined the inside. 'Bring a candle.'

Smithler passed one across. Kathryn held it carefully as she peered inside the skull. She studied the reddish glint on the top of the skull before reexamining each of the bones. She then pulled back the sleeve of her gown and searched in the cavity beneath the floorboards, scrabbling around till her hand grasped more dry bones.

'Faugh!' Smithler turned away in disgust at the remains of the skeletal hand which Kathryn brought out and laid gently on the floor.

'How long have these been here?' Colum asked.

Kathryn tapped the thin skull. 'Many years, perhaps even centuries. The bones have only remained intact because of the cavity beneath the floor.'

'Was someone buried here?' Colum asked.

Kathryn shook her head. 'I doubt it. These remains were probably hidden here. They are the tools of the black magician: the skull belongs to an executed felon, someone hanged on the gallows. As the victim strangles, blood vessels in the brain break and stain the skull. The hand'—she tapped it delicately—'is what the warlocks call the Hand of Glory. You cut it from a hanged man, preserve it carefully and when you wish to summon up the demons, put a candle made of human fat between the fingers.'

'So where did these come from?' Colum asked.

Kathryn brushed the dust and cobwebs from one of the bones.

'I suspect they belonged to the black magician who killed himself here: Erpingham's ancestor but, there again, it could have been anyone.'

'They caused the nightmares,' Sir Gervase declared from where he stood in the doorway. 'Can't you see, Mistress? Erpingham did see a ghost or some spectre from hell.'

'Nonsense,' Kathryn replied. 'This room may well have an evil history and a malevolent atmosphere but there must be a rational explanation, be it its choleric humours or some other natural cause, for the phantasm which plagued Erpingham's sleep.' She got to her feet, shaking the dust from her dress. 'Is there anything else?' she asked.

'No.'

Colum gestured at Standon to replace the floorboards as Kathryn went and sat on the edge of the bed.

'Please,' she asked abruptly. 'Could you all leave? Colum, put the key in the inside lock. I want to be alone as Erpingham was.'

The Irishman looked puzzled but obeyed. The guests, subdued, fearful of the allegations facing them, walked out into the gallery. Kathryn followed them to the door.

'Now, if I understand correctly,' she began, 'Sir Reginald came up here, carrying a goblet of wine.' She smiled and took Sir Gervase's goblet from his gnarled fingers. 'Then he locked the door.'

'Yes,' Standon replied. 'That's what happened.'

'No one came upstairs after Sir Reginald?'

'Well, I did,' Sir Gervase spoke up. 'But I went straight to my room.' He looked accusingly at the serjeant. 'You saw me do that. You came up the stairs after me, I'm sure you did!'

'Yes, yes, I did,' Standon replied. 'I was getting ready to stand on guard that night.'

Kathryn glanced at the serjeant.

'You are concealing something, aren't you, sir?' she asked sharply. 'You never told us you actually came up the stairs.'

Standon shuffled his feet; he ran his fingers nervously round the soiled collar of his tunic, scratching furiously at a pimple on his neck.

'Did you approach Sir Reginald?' Kathryn asked.

'I did,' Standon admitted. 'But . . .'

'Why didn't you tell us?' Colum snapped.

The serjeant's small, red-rimmed eyes blinked nervously.

'I was frightened,' he replied. 'Can't you see, I was the last man to speak to Sir Reginald.'

'What did happen?' Kathryn asked.

'I followed Sir Gervase up.' The serjeant pointed to his boots. 'These are soft leather, he would not have heard me. I wanted to make sure all was well after Sir Reginald's nightmare the previous evening. I tapped on his door. I said, "Sir Reginald, are you well?" He replied, "Yes, yes, now go away." '

'I didn't hear that,' Sir Gervase trumpeted.

'Well, I didn't shout,' Standon retorted. 'My boots are soft and, above all, Sir Reginald did not open the door.'

'Are you sure he was alone?' Kathryn asked.

Standon shrugged. 'Of course. Everyone else, apart from Sir Gervase, was downstairs.'

'Then what?' Kathryn asked.

'I went back to the taproom. I drank some more wine, everyone else went to bed. The tavern settled down for the night and that was it.'

'Fine,' Kathryn declared. 'Colum and the rest of you, just bear with me for a while.'

131

She went back into Erpingham's chamber and closed the door, flinching at the way it squeaked on its hinges. She turned the key and pulled across the bolts at the top and bottom. She noticed these were new, replacements after the door had been forced. She gazed round the sinister chamber, shivered, then irritably kicked the small pile of bones and skull still lying on the floor.

'Are you all right?' Colum called from the gallery.

'Yes, yes.' Kathryn smiled as she echoed Sir Reginald's words. She sat on the edge of the bed. 'What would I do?' she murmured, 'If I was he? I have brought my wine in so I put it down.' Kathryn got up, went round the bed and placed her cup on the table. 'The door was barred and locked. The window is shuttered, there are no secret entrances, no poisonous or noxious substances in the room. I undress, I throw my clothes on the floor.' Kathryn stared at the peg driven into the wall and scratched the side of her cheek. 'Why would he do that? Why not hang them up? Perhaps he was tired? I pause because Standon knocks on the door.' Kathryn rubbed her hands together. 'Of course I check the saddlebags. Or would I? They are strapped and buckled.' Kathryn stared up at the rafters and sighed noisily. 'A complete mystery. How was Erpingham poisoned and the bags of coins removed from his room?'

Kathryn went back to the door, drew back the bolts and unlocked it. She grimaced at Colum.

'No ghosts there but plenty of mystery. Let's visit Master Vavasour's room.'

They went farther along the gallery. Colum unlocked the room, they went in and he immediately unshuttered the window to provide more light. The chamber was smaller than Erpingham's though comfortably furnished with a four-poster bed, chair, stool, table and a chest at the foot of the bed for clothes. Kathryn opened this and went through Vavasour's meagre belongings: a change of clothes, a writing case, some rolls of parchment, a dagger in a battered sheath, but nothing remarkable. Colum pushed away the bed: Standon hurried forward to pick up the silver pieces lying there.

'Was Vavasour throwing his money about?' Kathryn asked.

'And there's one over here,' Lady Margaret exclaimed, picking up a coin.

'And here!' Tobias Smithler sifted amongst the rushes close to the wall near the door.

Standon was staring at the coins curiously.

'They're from the taxes!' he exclaimed.

'How can you be so sure?' Colum asked.

'They are freshly minted,' Standon asserted. 'Sir Reginald collected them from a merchant who had recently come from London. Look, Master Murtagh!'

Colum examined the coins. The silver was of good quality, not like the debased currency that had been circulating during the recent civil war.

'Is Standon correct?' Kathryn asked.

'Oh yes,' the Irishman replied. 'You see, the King defeated the last Lancastrian armies at the beginning of May. Not until the end of July did the Mint in the Tower begin to fashion new coins, the first time for a number of years. The King was able to use his enemies' estates and treasure to buy bullion from the Genoese.' He tossed a coin in his hand. 'I was responsible for some of this bullion being safely transported into London.'

'I never saw Vavasour with these coins,' Standon said excitedly. 'He must have taken them from the taxes.'

'Is this true?' Kathryn asked Smithler. 'Did Vavasour, or Sir Reginald, use such coins?'

The landlord examined the coin he was holding. 'No,' he said. 'This is the first time I have ever seen such a freshly minted piece. It's the new King's shilling.'

Colum beckoned with his fingers for all the coins to be handed over to him.

'It will be small consolation to the King,' he declared, 'that I can hand a little of his taxes back.' He put the silver into his purse then caught the look on Standon's face. 'Don't worry, man. These will find their way to the royal Exchequer.'

Colum then organised a thorough search of the room. One more coin was found at the far side of the bed but nothing else.

'How long will this go on?' Sir Gervase wailed as they reassembled in the taproom.

'How long is a piece of string?' Kathryn replied tartly.

She gazed back at the stairs. Something was wrong. Something she had seen in Vavasour's chamber.

'Kathryn?' Colum touched her gently on the arm.

'I don't think this is fair,' Father Ealdred complained. 'Vavasour's dead and some of the coins have been found in his chamber.'

'So?' Kathryn asked.

The lean-faced priest replied, 'It's obvious. Vavasour was party to the theft. Otherwise the coins would not have been found, would they?'

'How do you know they were not put there?' Colum asked.

'Impossible!' Smithler's mouth twisted in a sneer. 'The only person who had a key to that room was Vavasour. I never went in there. Did anyone else?'

A chorus of denials greeted his words.

'It's true,' Colum murmured.

Kathryn sat down on a chair. 'So you think Vavasour had an accomplice and they stole the money, though how is a mystery. They killed Erpingham, and that too is a mystery, then they quarrelled. If that is the case,' she continued flatly, 'why would Vavasour, who has his share of the money, go out in the dead of night and trek through an icy, snow-filled meadow to meet this accomplice? Why should he do that? According to you, the stolen coins must have been divided, otherwise Vavasour would not have dropped those coins.' She shook her head. 'It doesn't make sense. I can't accept that Vavasour, an accomplice to murder, treason and theft, would be so careless as to throw the proof of his crime around his chamber for anyone to see.' She shrugged at their silence. 'Somehow that money was placed there. Are you sure, Master Smithler, there's no second key to his chamber?'

The landlord threw up his hands in despair. 'Mistress Swinbrooke, you have lived in Canterbury many years. You know Forquil the locksmith? He lives not very far from you on the corner of Jewry Lane.'

'Yes, I know him,' Kathryn replied.

'Go and ask him. Last year he fashioned new locks for every chamber in this tavern. I wanted them strong and reliable. Forquil said he could only make one key for each lock, the mechanism is so refined and sensitive.'

'It's true,' Father Ealdred said. 'Mistress Swinbrooke, that's now the custom in many taverns. If a second key is fashioned, or there is a master key, the landlord or his servants are always blamed if anything is stolen.'

Kathryn just glanced despairingly at Colum; even before Father Ealdred's interruption, she knew the landlord was telling the truth. Because of the volume of pilgrim trade to Canterbury, landlords were eager to assure their customers that any possessions left in their chambers would be safe.

'So, how are the rooms cleaned?' Colum asked. 'Sheets and bedding changed?'

'We always do it when the guest is there,' Blanche Smithler explained. 'Ask any of the maids or slatterns. For God's sake, Master Murtagh, we have problems enough without allegations of theft being levelled against us, especially when we have no proof whether a customer is making a spurious claim or not.'

'So, no one goes near the bedchambers at all when the guests aren't there?' Colum insisted.

'Except to change the water in the fire buckets,' Blanche Smithler replied hastily. 'Hardly ever.'

Kathryn stared down at her hands. We are finished here, she thought; even this silver is a mystery. Vavasour's key was found in his wallet and so no one else could have entered his chamber. She swallowed hard. She dare not tell Colum that he would have to make a report to the King's Council at Westminster. She chewed the corner of her lip: there seemed to be no solution to this mystery. She closed her eyes and thought of Erpingham and then Vavasour's chamber.

'Who will bury Vavasour?' Smithler spoke up. 'I can't keep his corpse out in the stable for long.'

'Take it to the castle,' Colum ordered. 'He can be buried alongside his master.'

'Tell me.' Kathryn rose to her feet. 'After we left on our last visit here, did Vavasour say or do anything strange or untoward?'

'He kept to himself,' de Murville replied, 'which wasn't difficult. If we didn't like the master, we hardly had any respect for his servant.'

Kathryn looked at Standon.

'And you?'

'Vavasour hardly talked,' the serjeant replied. 'And, when he did, he was very keen on proverbs. You know, "A stitch in time saves nine." He said that to me once as I passed him on the stairs. On a couple of occasions, when I asked him about Erpingham's death, he smiled secretively and quoted the old adage, "There's many a slip 'twixt cup and lip." '

'And he didn't explain that?'

Standon shook his head.

Colum and Kathryn then made to leave, the Irishman repeating his instruction that everyone was to stay at the Wicker Man until his investigations were finished. He also told Smithler to burn the bones they'd found. Once they were outside, crossing the cobbled yard, Colum grasped Kathryn's hand.

'There is no solution, is there?' he asked.

Kathryn looked over her shoulder at the light-filled windows of the tavern.

'No,' she answered. 'This time, Colum, the murderer may well walk away scot free.'

Chapter 10

On their return to Ottemelle Lane, Kathryn and Colum spent the rest of Saturday having to cope with the effects of the thaw. The garden path had become flooded. A hole in the roof was discovered above the small garret Kathryn used as a storeroom, and the water butt was filled with dirty ice that slid off the red-tiled roof. Colum began to complain about having to go out to Kingsmead, wondering if Luberon had returned, so Kathryn had little opportunity to reflect on what she had learnt at the Wicker Man. At the same time she was concerned about Blunt and how she could tell Colum and Luberon the truth behind her suspicions.

Wormhair came round to see Kathryn, still clutching his stomach. He sat in the kitchen like some Jonah come to destruction, loudly protesting that he was on the verge of death.

'If you die,' Wuf shouted, 'can I have that wooden buckler you made last Michaelmas? And does that mean I can marry Agnes?'

The young maid became so aggrieved, Kathryn shooed Wuf away and took Wormhair into her chancery office. She carefully examined the young man.

'Well,' she declared gravely, pressing his stomach, then listening to it through a small pewter horn. 'The good news, Wormhair, is that you are not going to die, at least not yet.'

Wormhair just stared at her, his clear blue eyes even larger and rounder in his thin, pale face.

'But the pain?' he murmured.

'You have the flux?' Kathryn asked.

Wormhair nodded.

'And your bowels are very loose?'

A lugubrious groan answered her question.

'Well,' Kathryn added briskly, 'this is what comes of eating tainted meat. You should tell your master to give his apprentices something better. Now this is what you must do. First, never eat anything which smells suspiciously. Secondly, try to keep your hands clean. I don't know why, but my father always taught me that dirty fingers disturb the humours of the body. Now, I am going to give you a flask of sweetened water. Oh, yes, and don't eat anything until Monday morning.'

Wormhair's jaw fell.

'I mean that,' Kathryn insisted. 'Otherwise you will make your present complaint even worse.'

'And the medicine?' Wornhair asked expectantly.

'Wait here.' Kathryn went into her shop, then came back carrying a small phial. 'This is mugwort,' she explained. 'It can be found in any hedgerow. Now, mix it with the water, a few drops, then let it stand for about the space of five Aves. You take it in the morning, at noon and before you go to sleep. I promise you, this time tomorrow, you will feel much, much better.'

'I feel better now,' Wormhair replied.

Kathryn smiled. 'And just ignore Wuf. He speaks everything he thinks. He means well. God bless him, he has yet to understand what death means.'

Kathryn went back to the kitchen. Colum disappeared to his chamber. Wormhair left, saying he had to prepare the sanctuary for the morning Mass. An hour later Kathryn and her household ate their evening meal in relative silence, for they were all tired. After everyone had retired, Kathryn sat on the edge of her bed, slowly undressing. She paused and laughed softly. The last few days had been so busy; she and Colum had walked around like a man and wife who'd been married a lifetime. Nevertheless, she knew the Irishman was worried: Frenland's disappearance, the allegations of his waspish wife and the realisation that he might have to explain to the King about Erpingham and the lost taxes weighed heavily on his mind. Kathryn finished undressing. She put on a nightgown, doused the candles and sat for a while with the blankets heaped around her. She wondered about Erpingham. How had he been murdered and the taxes stolen from his room? What had Vavasour been doing out in that frozen meadow trying to cross an ice-covered mere? And, above all, what had she glimpsed in the dead clerk's room? Kathryn lay down and pulled the blankets over her head. She heard Thomasina come upstairs and the cheerful banter as she passed Colum in the gallery.

'Good night, oh sweetest and plumpest of them all!' the Irishman called.

'And good night to you, oh prince of liars!' Thomasina teased back.

Kathryn closed her eyes and drifted into sleep, Emma Darryl's face, strong and tear-stained, fresh in her mind.

The next morning she woke, feeling slightly heavy-headed after a restless night's sleep. Nevertheless, she roused the household; they dressed and went out into the icy street to St. Mildred's Church. They sat just inside the rood screen. Kathryn was pleased to see that Wormhair was looking better and, throughout Mass, kept winking slyly at Agnes, who shyly hid her face. Father Cuthbert preached a pithy sermon on the need for everyone to prepare for Christ's coming at Christmas. He made no reference to the deaths at Blunt's house, though Kathryn saw many of his congregation, like herself, gaze sadly at the unfinished painting behind the altar. Instead, Father Cuthbert emphasized the need for his parishioners to have their sins shriven and ensure harmony was maintained in the parish community. Colum had to hide his face behind his hand as the old but venerable priest stared pointedly at Widow Gumple who sat on a small stool in front of the altar steps, her ridiculous horn-shaped headdress up like a banner around her. Kathryn joined in the laughter when a few minutes later, as they took part in the offertory procession, Widow Gumple's headdress became snagged on the edge of a statue of St. Mildred and sent it rocking dangerously on its plinth. Gumple tried to extricate herself but this only made matters worse and the laughter grew as Wormhair dashed forward and, without being asked, pulled his knife from beneath his surplice and cut the good widow free.

The Mass ended in more merriment than Father Cuthbert would have liked. Afterwards Colum and Kathryn stayed in the churchyard with Father Cuthbert; he asked Kathryn to visit the Poor Priests' Hospital and enquired what plans she had for Christmas. The old priest kept blinking and coughing nervously.

'What is it, Father?' Kathryn asked. She grasped his vein-streaked hand. 'You are always telling me you have known me since I was knee-high to a daisy, which means I know you just as well.'

'It's not really you, Kathryn,' the old priest stammered, looking up at the dark-faced Irishman. 'I would like a word in private with Master Murtagh.'

Colum stared across the cemetery: Wuf and other children were shouting and screaming as they ran along a slide just beside the great wooden lychgate. Agnes was deep in conversation with Wormhair whilst Thomasina was volubly discussing the intricacies of Widow Gumple's headdress with other parishioners.

Colum smiled. 'This is as good a place as any, Father. Whatever you wish to say to me can be said in front of Mistress Swinbrooke.'

Kathryn hid her own nervousness: was Father Cuthbert going to question Colum about their private lives? As she had often said to Thomasina, people might wonder about Colum staying in her house but they had no right to draw any conclusions.

'Well, two things. First, for the Christmas crib may we have some straw and a manger? I heard of the building work out at Kingsmead. Perhaps . . .?'

'Yes, of course,' Colum interrupted. 'Anything you ask, Father. The second thing?'

Father Cuthbert's voice dropped. 'I notice you never take the Eucharist.'

140

Kathryn's stomach lurched: Colum went to the altar rails but only for a blessing; never did he take the bread and wine.

'I am sorry to ask,' Father Cuthbert stammered. 'But, but . . . I have a duty under God for the souls in my care.' He smiled weakly at Kathryn. 'Especially for a young woman whom I regard as more than a friend.'

Colum glanced away, staring up at the snarling face of a gargoyle carved above the church door. He watched a snowflake, dislodged from one of the sills, float gently down.

'I have had a violent past, Father,' Colum answered slowly.

'Yes, I know,' the priest exclaimed. 'They say you killed men. The reason I ask is, just before the snow fell, I was in London. I stayed at Blackfriars, and people there knew you. They said your own countrymen regard you as a traitor.'

'When I was young, Father, living outside the Pale of Dublin, I ran wild with a group of rebels and outlaws who called themselves the Hounds of Ulster, its name taken from one of the legends of old Ireland.' Colum's hand went beneath his cloak and he idly fondled the pommel of his dagger. 'To cut a long story short, Father, I and others were captured by the English. They went to the gibbet. I was pardoned because I was only a stripling. Now and again the Hounds of Ulster send assassins to kill me.' Colum pulled a face. 'So far I have been fortunate, I've killed every one.'

'But that was in self-defence,' Father Cuthbert insisted. 'There's no sin.'

'There are other things,' Colum murmured.

'I do not mean to pry,' Father Cuthbert apologised. 'But . . .' He glanced swiftly at Kathryn who was standing stock still, a vague suspicion forming in her mind. She abruptly shivered and knew it was not the bright winter morning.

'Have you ever been married, Master Murtagh?' Father Cuthbert's words came out in a rush.

'Yes,' Colum snapped.

Kathryn went so cold she felt dizzy.

'Master Murtagh.' The priest touched the Irishman's wrist. 'You may continue this conversation in a different place.'

'I was married,' Colum said slowly. 'A Welsh lass. We had a

boy.' Colum paused. 'In 1461, ten years ago, Father, I was with Lord Edward at Mortimer's Cross in the West Country. The Lancastrians landed a force in South Wales to ravage Lord Edward's estates. They attacked the village where my wife and child were staying. I came back to find my life a smoking ruin. On a morning very like this, I buried them in the cold, hard earth and, at the time, I cursed God with every breath.' He glanced at the priest. 'So, that is why I do not partake of the Eucharist.' The Irishman's face became hard. 'I attend Mass, as church law says, but I'll only go back to the sacraments when the hate has been cleaned from my heart.' He stared into the priest's kindly face then clapped him gently on the shoulder. 'And don't worry, Father. You were right to ask. No offence has been given and none has been taken.' He linked his arm through Kathryn's. 'And you have my word, Father. This Christmas you will have the finest crib ever!'

Father Cuthbert blessed them and left whilst they walked down through the lychgate. Thomasina gathered from Kathryn's face that something had upset her, so she stayed behind to shout at Wuf and Agnes to join her.

'Why didn't you tell me?' Kathryn asked softly. She glanced up at Colum. 'You must have been quite young?'

'Aye and a great romantic.' Colum squeezed her hand. 'I never talk about it, Kathryn. There are certain rooms in everyone's soul which are best kept locked. I loved the lass and she loved me. I never thought it would happen. I was with Lord Edward on the Welsh march. There was a Lancastrian army in the Midlands and North, then the Bretons landed from the sea and marched through South Wales, burning and pillaging. We caught up with them at Mortimer's Cross a few miles north of Hereford.' Colum's voice became hard. 'We won the battle. Very few of the Bretons were taken prisoner. I have done my share of killing,' he added. 'And all it does is beget more.'

'Is that why you keep the chest in your room locked?' Kathryn asked.

'Mementoes.' Colum squeezed her hand. 'Bits and pieces of a

former life.' Colum stopped and stared narrow-eyed at her. 'Now you know I am a dreadful man.' He pushed his face closer. 'A wicked, evil beast,' he teased. 'A ravisher of maids.'

'Watch your step, Irishman!' Thomasina called, coming up behind him.

Kathryn was glad of the interruption as was Colum, who immediately started to quote phrases about Thomasina's maiden feet and how

'Like Candace in The Squire's Tale
Thomasina sauntered at an easy pace.'

Kathryn let the teasing and banter pass by her. One more piece, she thought, to the puzzle behind this Irishman. He was now hiding his own hurt behind the banter with Thomasina: he smiled and chattered, but his body was stiff with tension. Kathryn quietly vowed she would never refer to Colum's long-dead wife unless he wanted to. Any further reflection ended as soon as they reached home. Thomasina took over the kitchen, loudly declaring, 'To roast pork in caraway sauce is a skill best left to me alone!'

Kathryn went to her writing chamber whilst Colum, eager not to be questioned any further, went out to watch Wuf play in the garden. Kathryn still wondered about the Irishman. What other secrets did he hold? She felt embarrassed at her nagging curiosity. Who was she to condemn anyone? After all, she had secrets which, as a city official, she had a duty to make public. Yet what could she do? She wandered back down the passageway to the kitchen door. Wuf was beside the carp pond, sliding his polished wooden disc across the ice, knocking down stacks of pebbles.

'Be careful, Wuf,' Kathryn warned. 'Colum, for God's sake, the ice is melting and the water's cold enough to kill!'

She watched Wuf play under Colum's careful tutelage and abruptly recalled Vavasour walking out across the frozen mere. An idea occurred to her.

'No!' Kathryn whispered. 'That's ridiculous!'

She stepped out into the garden but then hurriedly returned at a loud, insistent knocking on the front door. Agnes went to answer and Luberon, red-cheeked, his eyes glittering, strolled down the passage as grandly as a bishop.

'Mistress Swinbrooke, good day. Where is Master Murtagh?' The little man positively quivered with excitement.

'What do you want?' Thomasina asked archly. 'Like any man, you can smell a good meal a mile away!'

Luberon handed Agnes his cloak and rubbed his hands in glee. He closed his eyes and savoured the fragrance of the roasting pork.

'Oh, Thomasina, you'd not turn a poor man away? Surely the best cook in Canterbury has a morsel for poor Luberon?'

Thomasina turned away, blushing. Colum, drawn by the noise, came into the kitchen.

'You have found Frenland, haven't you?' Kathryn asked.

Luberon's eyes almost popped out of his head. 'How did you know?'

Kathryn smiled and invited him to sit at the table where Agnes was setting out the platters.

'Come on, Simon, join us for dinner. Colum.' Kathryn waved the Irishman to the head of the table.

Colum sat down and stared quizzically at Kathryn. 'You mean to say you knew Frenland was not dead?'

'Of course,' Kathryn laughed. 'First, wild dogs can be dangerous but not that dangerous. They'll hunt a child or a wounded animal but not a fully grown man. Secondly, Frenland hadn't far to go. According to the map, the road he fled down leads to a number of villages and hamlets. Thirdly, I was intrigued how he questioned you about Alexander Wyville. I think that gave him the idea.'

'For what?' Colum asked.

'For running away from a shrewish wife.' Kathryn laughed self-consciously. 'Frenland does have another woman, doesn't he, Simon?'

'Yes, yes. A rosy-cheeked, pert-eyed widow.' Luberon raised his voice. 'A lot like you, Thomasina.'

'Watch your tongue!' The red-faced cook warned laughingly.

144

'Finally,' Kathryn concluded, 'I looked at the blood-soaked, tattered cloak. I found scraps of leather, very similar to that of a wine skin. What Frenland did was fill such a leather pouch with animal blood, which can be easily bought at a slaughterhouse. He took his cloak and sprinkled it with blood and away he goes. I found traces of the leather pannikin amongst the ragged remains of his cloak.'

She took the cup of posset Thomasina placed on the table and passed it to Luberon. The little clerk sighed and sipped appreciatively.

'When I found Frenland,' he declared, 'I informed him about his wife's allegations.' Luberon grinned. 'It's a private, civil matter between the two, or should I say three of them.'

Colum leaned back in his chair and laughed softly. 'Oh, by all that is holy, how complicated life can become!' He patted Luberon on the arm.

Kathryn studied the clerk who kept looking down at the leather bag which he'd brought with him. 'There's something else, isn't there, Simon?'

Luberon put the cup down on the table. 'Blunt's dead,' he remarked quietly.

Kathryn whirled round as Thomasina dropped a dish to clatter against the stone hearth.

'He died during the night,' Luberon continued. 'He just slipped away. The guards came to rouse him; leaning against the cell wall he was, eyes closed. I've been to tell Emma Darryl.' He looked over his shoulder at Thomasina. 'Oh, by the way,' he added, 'the prisoner never ate or drank what you left him.' He opened the leather bag and drew out a small linen-covered bundle.

Kathryn took and opened it carefully. The bread and cheese were now stale, but the little purse of powder Thomasina had slipped in was still tightly bound. Kathryn picked up a knife, cut the cord and sniffed at the powder.

'It's valerian!' Kathryn exclaimed.

'I know,' Thomasina replied, coming over. 'Not enough to kill, Mistress, but sufficient to keep him drugged. I also know how he died. I went to see Blunt's old physician.' She smiled faintly at Kathryn. 'Someone you know, Roger Chaddedon. He sends his regards and hopes to see you over the Christmas season.'

Kathryn blushed. Chaddedon was a widower who, much to Colum's annoyance, made no attempt to disguise his deep liking for Kathryn.

'What did he say?' Kathryn asked, trying to avoid Colum's eye.

'That he met Blunt on the feast of All Souls and examined him carefully. He had, at the very most, a few weeks to live. His lungs were rotting, coughing up black blood. Chaddedon thought this was caused by the paint and other noxious substances Blunt had used over the years. I am sorry about the valerian, Mistress, but no man should experience the full horrors of hanging, especially someone like Blunt.'

Kathryn turned to Luberon. 'And you have told Emma Darryl?'

'Yes.'

'What did she say?'

'Very little. She smiled faintly but then said something strange: "You must go because I have to prepare something to eat." '

Kathryn started, and a cold shiver ran up her spine.

'Thomasina, we will not be eating now. Colum, Luberon, quickly, get your cloaks!'

'What's the matter?' Colum exclaimed.

'We have to see Emma Darryl!' Kathryn snapped, rising to her feet.

Colum grabbed her arm. 'Why?'

Kathryn took a deep breath and looked apologetically at Luberon.

'Because Blunt did not kill Alisoun or her two suitors!'

'That's ridiculous!' the Irishman said. 'We saw the arrow wounds. Blunt, by his own confession, was a master archer.'

Kathryn shook her head as she wrapped her cloak about her.

Mistress Swinbrooke, what are you saying?' Luberon rose to his feet, draining his posset cup and looking round for his cloak. Agnes and Wuf were now standing in the doorway of the kitchen, watching and listening expectantly.

'I'll tell you as we walk,' Kathryn murmured.

They left the house a few minutes later and hurried up Ottemelle Lane. Apart from the wandering dogs, the occasional beggar and a desperate red-wigged whore looking for custom, the streets were deserted. The sun was beginning to dip. The air had grown colder and the soiled snow was now dirty ice. Once they crossed Church Lane, Kathryn slowed down.

'Colum.' She grasped the Irishman's arm to steady herself. 'Blunt was a master archer but his eyesight was poor and he had that terrible cough. How could he have pulled a bow, taken aim and released three arrows so swiftly? For heaven's sake,' she continued, 'Alisoun and her two suitors, Nicholas and Absolon, would have heard him coming from a mile away.'

'But the arrow wounds?' Luberon asked, coming up beside her.

'Yes, the arrow wounds,' Kathryn said. 'They were very deep. This is what happened,' she continued, hurrying on. 'Blunt came home and found Alisoun and her two admirers poisoned. He wanted to protect Emma Darryl. He took his bow and shot an arrow into each of the corpses and, to make it look more realistic, opened a window, probably waited for someone like Widow Gumple, and threw Nicholas's corpse out.'

'And you can tell that?' Colum asked. 'Just from the arrow wounds?'

'Yes, they were far too deep and don't forget how dark that chamber was at Blunt's house. A young man, a professional archer, would have been able to deliver three killing arrows. Perhaps if he had been in good health, Blunt could have done the same, but not racked by coughs, his eyesight failing.'

'Why didn't you tell us?' Colum accused.

Kathryn stopped and stared at the large icicles forming on the porch of the large house.

'How could I?' she said softly. 'When I visited Blunt in his prison cell, he was dying. That's why he asked to see me. He was no fool. He knew I would be called to examine the corpses. Now the light in the death house was poor but something about the skin of each corpse, the wet spongy feeling and the slight discolouration made me think.' She shook the water from her cloak.

'The arrow wounds were so deep, so precise, only a master archer, loosing at very close range, could have inflicted them. The man we met in the guildhall dungeon, with his squinting eyes and racking cough, could never have achieved that.' Kathryn wetted her lips. 'Neither Peter nor Emma possessed such skill, so I reached the conclusion that Emma killed all three before Blunt ever returned home.'

'And now you intend to confront her?'

Kathryn shook her head. 'No, I want to save Peter. Lord save us, I hope I am not too late!'

They took a short cut down an alleyway to Blunt's house. Kathryn, her stomach heaving, hands slightly trembling, hammered on the door. With a sigh of relief she heard ponderous footsteps and the bolts being pulled back. The door swung open, and Peter stood there smiling at them.

'Peter,' Kathryn cried, pushing him to one side. 'Are you well?'

'I am hungry,' the young man replied. 'And Emma should be up making dinner, but she is still fast asleep.'

Kathryn pushed by him and hurried up the stairs to the second gallery, Colum and Luberon thundering behind her. She glimpsed a half-open door and went into the bedchamber. Emma Darryl was lying on the bed, hands by her side, her eyes staring sightlessly up at the canopy. Kathryn sat down and grasped the woman's hand. She felt a slight tinge of warmth but no blood flow in the neck or wrists. She then pressed her ear against the thick, woollen dress but could detect no heartbeat. Kathryn stared round the chamber as Colum and Luberon burst in. She pointed to a small silver dish standing on an iron-bound chest.

'Colum, bring that here, quickly!'

Colum passed this over. Kathryn polished the silver plate with the cuff of her sleeve and held it as close as possible to the woman's lips. She took it away and crossed herself.

'Dead?' Colum asked.

'Aye, God rest her. Master Luberon, ask Peter to stay downstairs.'

Luberon walked out of the gallery. Kathryn heard him speaking softly; then he came back, closing the door behind him. Kathryn gazed at Murtagh.

'We have all got secrets, Irishman, haven't we?'

Colum recalled his conversation with Father Cuthbert and nodded slightly.

'And you, Master Luberon, know mine. I constantly wonder if my husband is really dead or, one day, might return.' Kathryn gently stroked the dead woman's hand. 'Well, Emma Darryl had her secrets.' Kathryn's eyes never left Colum. 'She loved Richard Blunt with a consuming passion. They had a child, a boy named Peter, but they never married. Blunt, as we'll call him even though it wasn't his baptismal name, had three great gifts. First, as an archer, secondly as a painter, and thirdly, his loyal Emma: where he went, Emma accompanied him.' Kathryn stared round the comfortable chamber and steeled herself against the sheer pathos of the tragedy.

'Now Blunt fell ill, just a cough to begin with, but as he breathed in the noxious humours from the materials he used in his paintings at St. Mildred's and elsewhere, it grew worse. His life began to slip away and then he met Alisoun, a true May and December romance. Matters might have remained calm and peaceful but Alisoun played the harlot, hastening Blunt's death. Emma Darryl watched this and silently brooded.' Kathryn looked down at the dead woman's face, so peaceful in death. 'Emma feared Alisoun with her menacing threats against herself and, more acutely, against her son Peter. She also became alarmed: Blunt was going to die and Alisoun, his wife, would inherit everything. She and Peter would be turned out of doors, left to beg.'

'So Emma killed Alisoun?'

'Yes. I doubt very much if Emma also intended to kill the two young men. Yet you can imagine the scene. Blunt was in St. Mildred's and Alisoun was here whilst Emma, the faithful housekeeper, prepared a deadly potion.' Kathryn picked up the wine cup from the table at the side of the bed and sniffed, wrinkling her nose at its acrid stench. 'I suspect Emma used what the Latins term *Amanita virosa,* a deadly mushroom. The cap is egg-shaped, silky white, glossy, tinged at the centre to a foxy brown.'

Kathryn took the wine cup across the chamber and poured the dregs into a night jar.

'It makes a deadly potion which can be hidden beneath the strong tang of claret. On the night of the murder, Emma retired to bed as Alisoun entertained two visitors and shared her wine with them. Perhaps Emma sat in this chamber listening to their laughter: she was past caring, so consumed with hate against Alisoun. Then Blunt returned and discovered the three corpses.'

'And he took the blame?' Luberon interjected.

'Oh yes. Peter was probably sent to his chamber whilst Blunt began this play-acting with the bow and arrow. He would reason with Emma, point out that he was going to die anyway. She would have to stay to look after Peter.'

'And would Emma agree to that?'

'Perhaps, reluctantly; that's why Blunt demanded to see me—he wanted to make sure his sacrifice had not been in vain.' Kathryn walked to the window and stared out over the ice-covered rooftops. 'As soon as I met him in the cell at the guildhall I knew something was wrong. The same was true when I studied his painting at St. Mildred's, of Abraham sacrificing Isaac on the altar. Did you notice the knife was turned inwards? Abraham's preparing to sacrifice himself rather than his son. Blunt was thinking of himself.'

'But that was done before the murders, wasn't it?' Luberon asked.

Kathryn looked over her shoulder. 'I wonder,' she replied. 'Did Blunt know the murders were going to occur? Or did he see himself dying because of his work, sacrificing himself for his family?' Kathryn gestured at the bed. 'Whatever, as soon as Blunt died, Emma had no reason to live. She may have suspected that we knew the truth and so the poor woman took her own life.' Kathryn turned round and leant against the windowsill. 'When Simon told me that her reaction to Blunt's death was to wonder about what to eat, she was already planning her own death. I just prayed that she would entrust Peter to our care and compassion.

Anyway, it's over,' Kathryn concluded. 'Simon, please take Peter to Father Cuthbert at the Poor Priests' Hospital. Explain what has happened, then come back and seal the house.'

Luberon agreed. Kathryn heard him go down the stairs and talk to Peter, then the door closed as they left the house. Kathryn walked over and grasped Colum's hands.

'The past can be dreadful,' she said softly. 'It's never really the past but, like a shadow, hangs close behind you. Sometimes it just catches you up in its dark embrace. We must not let that happen to us.'

Colum bent down and gently kissed her on the lips. Kathryn blushed and stepped back.

'One less secret,' she murmured, pointing at the bed.

'And the business at the Wicker Man?' Colum asked.

Kathryn drew in a deep breath and walked briskly towards the door. She paused, her hand on the latch.

'God be my witness, Irishman. I don't know, except that there may be some mysteries which are never resolved.'

Chapter 11

They returned home. Thomasina had the meal ready and Kathryn ate in silence, still affected by the deaths of Blunt and Emma Darryl. She quietly vowed to visit Father Cuthbert and ensure that Peter remained in kind hands whilst any property and monies the simpleton might inherit were properly handled. Colum ate quickly, then went up to his own chamber; he could see that Kathryn was lost in her own thoughts so he cheerfully hid his own frustration and disappointment. In his mind, he was already beginning to draft what he would write to the King's Exchequer in London about Erpingham's and Vavasour's murders.

Outside darkness began to fall though Wuf still insisted on playing in the garden, so Kathryn absent-mindedly let him. As Thomasina and Agnes cleared the table, Kathryn went back to her chancery. She lit a lantern and a few candles, prepared parchment and quill and began to list her thoughts and suspicions about Erpingham's murder and Vavasour's mysterious death in the frozen mere. Kathryn nibbled the end of the quill. What was it, she thought, that she had seen amiss in Vavasour's chamber? She heard Wuf shrieking with laughter in the garden so, clutching the lantern, she went out to discover what was happening. She found him on the edge of the small carp pond, sliding his polished wooden disc across, then running round to the other side to collect it. He was in no danger so Kathryn stood for a while watching him.

Wuf shouted at her. 'Soon the ice will crack!'

Kathryn smiled and made her way towards him. Wuf sent the disc spinning across; sure enough, the ice beneath, warming under the thaw, crackled and snapped. Kathryn put the lantern down on the edge of the pond so Wuf could see more clearly.

'Sooner or later, sooner or later,' Wuf chorused, 'the ice will crack!'

'Wuf!' Thomasina called from the kitchen. 'Come in here and help!'

The little boy looked at Kathryn.

'Go on, Wuf!'

She took him by the hand and led him to the kitchen door. Wuf scampered in. Kathryn walked back to collect the lantern, then abruptly stopped. She saw the light and the wooden disc, and her heart leapt.

'Of course!' she breathed. 'That explains it!'

Kathryn stared at the lantern. Vavasour's death had been a mystery. Everyone had been in the tavern, yet someone must have been waiting on the mere for Erpingham's clerk to come. But how had that person survived when Vavasour had drowned in the frozen waters? She gingerly made her way down the garden path, picked up the lantern and wooden disc and hastened back into the kitchen. She ignored Thomasina's questioning glance and Wuf's request that his toy be returned. Instead she returned to her writing office. She picked up her quill and quickly drew a rough sketch of the Great Meadow, indicating with a cross where Raston had seen the light flickering, inviting Vavasour forward onto the mere. Kathryn put the quill down and leaned back, steepling her fingers.

'If that's how it was done,' she said to herself, 'the next question is who had the means and resources to set such a trap?'

She took out a list of the people at the Wicker Man.

'There can only be one conclusion. But how does this resolve Erpingham's death?' She remembered the grisly skull and bones found under the floorboards: how had they caused Erpingham's nightmare? Kathryn took down her father's battered folio, greasy with age and thumb marks, which listed all known poisons. Each entry had been filled in at different times and only careful scrutiny of the faded inked pages found the entry on deadly nightshade. Kathryn smiled sadly as she read the entry.

'A tall herb,' her father had written, 'which can survive all year and has many branched stems. The flowers are purple, solitary and drooping though sometimes they can be lurid violet or violet-green. Its fruit, shining black berries, is a great danger to children and the unwary. The drug is distilled either from fresh or dried leaves or roots, though all parts of this herb are poisonous. Nevertheless, it is very useful in resolving the evil humours of the stomach, but even small quantities can cause severe poisoning.'

Kathryn finished reading the entry and was about to close the folio when she noticed a further entry, the ink very faded, scrawled in the margin. She pulled the lantern closer yet; even under its light, the writing remained illegible. She took a large magnifying glass from a small coffer, went back and studied the cramped letters. Her father had written in shorthand but Kathryn, flushed with excitement, could decipher it. She put the glass down and leaned back in the chair, closed the folio and clasped it in her hands.

'Thank you,' she whispered: that simple entry had helped resolve one mystery. 'You don't know as much as you think you do, Swinbrooke,' Kathryn murmured. 'Perhaps it's time you reread all your father's journals.'

Kathryn closed her eyes and tried to recall every detail surrounding Erpingham's death. How the tax collector had eaten and drunk only what the other guests had. How he had taken his goblet upstairs to his chamber, locking and barring the door. No one had approached him except for Standon, who wished to ensure all was well with his master.

'But he never checked the taxes?' Kathryn murmured, opening her eyes. 'His clothes were thrown in a heap. No poison was found in his room. How was that done, eh?'

Kathryn already had a vague suspicion about the identity of the assassin, but how was the crime carried out? She closed her eyes again: Vavasour; his chamber; the coins lying on the floor.

'Kathryn?'

She started. Colum stood in the doorway, staring strangely at her.

'You shouldn't be so soft-footed, Irishman.'

Colum sat on a stool beside Kathryn's desk; he noticed how her cheeks were slightly flushed, her eyes sparkling.

'You've found something, haven't you?' he asked quickly. He grabbed her hand and squeezed it. 'I knew you would, oh clever physician.'

Kathryn replied carefully. 'I may know how Vavasour died. He was lured to his death but, at the moment, that's not important.'

'What is, then?'

'The details concerning Erpingham's death.' She tapped her father's folio. 'I have just discovered there were two distinct attempts to kill Erpingham.'

'Two!' Colum exclaimed.

'Oh yes. I have just read my father's journal on poisons. Deadly nightshade is well named. It causes death very quickly: a heavy sleepiness and the victim slips away quietly.' Kathryn tapped the folio again. 'But a few grains of deadly nightshade will have another effect: it might not kill but it will cause fantasies in the mind, delirium and nightmares.'

'And so Erpingham was given the potion twice?'

'Yes. Just think, there he is, a godless man, sleeping in a chamber where, according to legend, one of his ancestors, a devil worshipper, had died. Now Erpingham would reflect deeply upon that, perhaps even revel in it. However, the night before he died, he was given a few grains of deadly nightshade, not enough to kill, but certainly sufficient to evoke a horrid nightmare. Do you remember what Sir Gervase told us about Erpingham's appearance? Flushed face, sweaty, feeling of nausea, his limbs trembling? Well, those are the effects of a few grains of deadly nightshade.' Kathryn paused. 'Now, what I think happened is that Erpingham fell asleep and the potion set to work. Our tax collector suffered a mild delirium. Now either he has a dream or, waking up, cannot distinguish between what he saw in his sleep and what his potion-soaked imagination made him see. Anyway, Erpingham rises from his bed. He is agitated and nervous and goes next door. Gervase gives him some wine. Erpingham is sick either before he visits Percy or afterwards, and this purges his body of the evil humours caused by the poison.' Kathryn sighed. 'The following night Erpingham is not so fortunate: this time the murderer realises his mistake and increases the strength. Erpingham dies and our mystery is set.'

'But who?' Colum asked. 'How and why?'

'For that,' Kathryn declared. 'I am going to need everyone in this house. Colum, before I lay allegations against anyone, I wish to see if I can play the same trick the murderer did.' She leaned forward and stroked the Irishman gently on the cheek. 'Please ask Thomasina, Agnes and Wuf to gather in the kitchen. Tell Thomasina to get three of our pewter wine cups down. You know, the ordinary sort.'

Colum opened his mouth to ask further questions.

'Go on,' Kathryn urged. 'And, if I am right, before the day is finished, we will return to the Wicker Man tavern to trap the murderer.'

Colum needed no further encouragement: he hurried into the passageway calling for Thomasina and the rest. They all gathered around the kitchen table. Thomasina was intrigued, Wuf and Agnes only too glad to be called away from their household tasks.

Kathryn sat down in her chair.

'Now, Thomasina,' she began, 'please fill the wine cupss.'

Thomasina picked up the flagon and obeyed.

'Keep a cup for yourself,' Kathryn urged. 'Give one to Colum and the last to me.' Kathryn sipped from hers. 'Come on,' she teased. 'Aren't you going to drink my health?'

Colum raised his eyebrows at Thomasina and they both drank. For a while Kathryn just sat, sipping at her wine cup.

'You always were the mysterious one!' Thomasina exclaimed.

Kathryn smiled back. 'Thomasina, I have a task for you. Take your wine cup up to my chamber and trim the hour candle there.'

'Trim the hour candle?' Thomasina retorted. 'What on earth has got into you, Mistress? You're acting like a flibbertigibbet!'

'Thomasina, please do exactly what I say.'

The nurse, breathing noisily, picked up a sharp knife and, with the wine cup in her other hand, went dolefully along the passageway and up the stairs.

'What's going to happen?' Wuf asked, eyes shining. 'Can Agnes and I have some wine?'

'No, you can't,' Kathryn snapped. 'Just sit still and be patient.' She leaned over and tapped the little boy on the nose. 'But tomorrow, Wuf, I am going to take you to the baker's and buy you the largest marzipan slice he has on his stall. You too, Agnes,' Kathryn added quickly, seeing the disappointment in the maid's eyes.

'And what about me?' Colum asked.

Kathryn's face became mock-serious. 'Oh yes, and you can have some marzipan too.'

'I'm trimming the bloody candle!' Thomasina bellowed from the bedchamber. 'Are you going to leave me here forever, Mistress?'

Kathryn smiled, picked up her wine cup and, putting her finger to her lips as a sign for the rest to be quiet, went quickly along the passageway and up the stairs.

'What's this all about?' Agnes whispered to Colum.

'I don't know,' Colum replied. 'But we'll eventually find out.'

In a few minutes, Kathryn, followed by a still grumbling Thomasina, reentered the kitchen.

'What was that all about?' Thomasina muttered, sitting down. 'Mistress, you know I trim the candles first thing every morning!'

'Drink your wine,' Kathryn urged.

Thomasina slurped from the cup.

'It is your wine?'

Thomasina looked at the cup. 'Of course.'

'No, it isn't,' Kathryn pointed out. 'Look at the cup, Thomasina. On one side you'll find a faint scar, probably where Wuf dropped it.'

Thomasina examined the cup carefully. 'Yes, yes, I can see it.'

'Now, I had that cup before I went upstairs. I followed you into the bedchamber. You put your cup on the table, didn't you?'

'Well, yes of course, I . . .'

'All I did,' Kathryn explained, 'was exchange your cup for mine. If I'd put poison in mine, you would be well on your way to heaven's high towers.'

'Oh, Lord save us!' Thomasina clucked. 'You give me the shivers!'

'Is that what happened at the Wicker Man?' Colum asked.

'Perhaps,' Kathryn replied. 'But we have another small game to play.' She looked at the little maid. 'Agnes, can you count?'

'Oh, yes,' the girl replied. 'I can count to forty on my fingers, though any higher, I'll need a checkerboard.'

'Good!' Kathryn declared. 'Then go to the foot of the stairs, sit on the stool and tell me who goes upstairs and how many times.'

'Can I do that?' Wuf shouted; then his face became serious. 'But I can only count to ten!'

'You can help us,' Kathryn soothed.

Agnes obeyed and, with Thomasina grumbling that she had better things to do, the rest of the household began to troop up and down the stairs.

'Now, remember, Agnes,' Kathryn declared. 'I only want you to notice who goes upstairs and how many times.'

Wuf loved it and went scampering up and down like a whippet. Thomasina followed more ponderously, Colum was bemused, and Kathryn was ensuring that Agnes was counting. After a few minutes, Kathryn came down and gestured for Agnes to stop.

'How many times did I go up? How many times did I go up?' Wuf danced from foot to foot.

Agnes closed her eyes. 'Wuf went up six times, no, I think seven. Master Murtagh five; yourself, Mistress, twice. Thomasina, twice or was it three times?'

'Good!' Kathryn exclaimed. 'And how many times did we come down?'

Agnes's eyes flew open. 'But you didn't ask me that!' she cried. 'You told me to count how many times people went *up* the stairs.'

'And where's Thomasina?' Kathryn asked.

'I am at the top of the stairs,' Thomasina shouted. 'Where you told me to be, Mistress!'

'Kathryn!' Colum exclaimed, a note of exasperation in his voice. 'What is all this about?'

'A simple game, Irishman. Agnes was so intent on remembering who went up the stairs, she failed to take proper count of who came down. Remember, we asked the same question of the guests at the Wicker Man? Now the rest of you must be patient. Colum, collect your cloak and mine. Oh, you'd best take your sword belt as well. Agnes, go across to the tavern on the corner.' She handed the maid a coin. 'Give this to one of the pot boys and tell him to go straight to the guildhall. He's to ask Master Luberon to join us at the Wicker Man.' Kathryn smiled at Thomasina and patted her on the shoulder. 'I promise, I'll explain everything on our return.'

By the time they arrived at the Wicker Man, Kathryn had explained her conclusions and how she was to prove them. They found the taproom empty, the guest having retired to their chambers.

'Oh, not again!' Tobias Smithler moaned as Colum and Kathryn came through the door. 'Mistress Swinbrooke, I have a living to make.'

'Aye,' Kathryn replied. 'But the King's Justices, not to mention God's, wait for an answer.'

The landlord looked at her strangely.

'I want everyone down here!' Colum interrupted. 'All the guests and your servant Raston. Once they are, the doors of the tavern are to be locked, the servants confined to their quarters and the keys handed over to me.'

Smithler was about to object, but Colum drew his dagger and drove it quiveringly into the tabletop.

'I am the King's Commissioner,' the Irishman warned, making even Kathryn start. 'You, sir, will do as you are told!' Colum pointed at the taverner's pallid-faced wife. 'And you, Mistress Blanche, will serve us some wine.'

Colum arranged the trestle tables, pushing two together with benches along each side. As the guests hurried down, the Irishman gestured to Kathryn to sit at the head of the table.

'I will sit by your side.' Colum pulled the dagger from the tabletop and sat on a stool, slipping the dagger into the top of his boot.

'Sweet heavens above!' Sir Gervase trumpeted, taking his place. 'No rest for the wicked, eh?' He wagged one bony finger at the Irishman. 'I don't care if you are an angel sent by the good Lord. Tomorrow morning, if this thaw continues, I am leaving. You know where my manor house is. You can send your bailiffs there to arrest me.'

Sir Gervase's words were chorused by the rest.

Colum gazed unblinkingly back. The old knight lost some of his bombast and hid his embarrassment by gulping from his wine cup.

'We really must go,' Lady Margaret de Murville said. 'Master Murtagh, Mistress Swinbrooke, not every mystery under heaven can be solved. I am innocent, as is my husband, of any crime. Christmas will soon be upon us. The roads are difficult to traverse . . .' Her voice trailed off.

'I shall not keep you long,' Kathryn declared.

She paused as Raston, the last to arrive, came lumbering in. He gave Kathryn a gap-toothed grin and sat on a stool at the far corner of the table. Colum pointed at Smithler.

'Sir, your keys?'

The landlord almost threw them along the table. Colum put them on the floor next to him.

'Mistress Swinbrooke,' the Irishman murmured. 'Everyone will now listen to what you have to say.'

'Vavasour,' Kathryn began. 'Poor old Vavasour, Erpingham's clerk. You will remember he went out to the Great Meadow to meet someone? He went down the hill, attracted by that beacon light winking through the mist, inviting him onto the mere, which broke and drowned him.'

'Aye, that's correct,' Raston confirmed. 'I see what I sees.' The old poacher glared round fiercely, daring anyone to object.

160

'Now, you may also remember,' Kathryn continued, 'that this was a great mystery, for everyone was in the tavern when Vavasour left. Secondly, if the ice broke beneath him, why didn't it also drag down the murderer waiting there? Thirdly, we found no sign of the assassin either going down to the mere or returning.' She looked at the landlord's wife. 'Mistress Blanche, I would like a large metal plate, thin and smooth.'

The taverner's wife just stared at her.

'Please,' Kathryn insisted. 'Do as I say.'

The woman hurried to obey. She brought back a large plate. Kathryn inspected its base, running her hand over the smooth metal. She pointed down the table at Sir Gervase.

'Sir,' she exclaimed. 'Get ready to catch this!'

The old knight looked startled.

'No,' Kathryn laughed. 'I am not going to throw it but just slide it down the table towards you.'

Father Ealdred, who was sitting where the two tables joined, pulled them closer together. Kathryn pulled the plate back and sent it skimming along the table towards the old knight, who neatly caught it.

'Now,' Kathryn invited, 'send it back to me.'

The old knight obliged and the plate clattered along the table into Kathryn's hands.

'What does this prove?' Lord de Murville declared.

'I know,' Raston said. 'When I was young, I'd go down to the River Stour when it was frozen and do the same with the polished shinbone of an ox.'

'Exactly,' Kathryn breathed. 'And that's what happened the night poor Vavasour died.'

'What did?' Father Ealdred asked. 'Mistress Swinbrooke, I cannot follow your line of thought.'

Kathryn took a lantern from a shelf and put it on the plate.

'Father, somebody took a lantern and a large plate, something like this, a platter or bowl made of pewter or bronze. They crossed the Great Meadow, lit the lantern, put it on the platter and pushed it out across the mere.' Kathryn tapped the plate. 'Something like this, though I suspect it was a bowl with a slightly raised edge to prevent the lantern sliding off. Vavasour's assassin put the lighted lantern into the bowl and, using a pole, pushed it across the frozen ice. The murderer then carried that pole back to the Wicker Man.'

'But that's ridiculous!' Standon snapped.

Kathryn studied the soldier's unshaven face. 'Why is it ridiculous?' she asked.

'Well, first, the person would have been seen.'

'No, they would not,' Kathryn interrupted. 'On a dark, freezing night anyone could have slipped out with a lantern hooked on their belt, a tinder in their pouch and a bronze platter or bowl beneath their cloak.'

The serjeant pulled a face and nodded.

'But surely,' Father Ealdred objected, 'surely Raston or Vavasour would have seen that the lantern wasn't held by someone?'

'Would they?' Colum interrupted. 'The night was cold and misty. Remember, Raston and Vavasour stood on the top of the hill looking downwards. Have you ever seen a lantern shine through a night mist? It shimmers deceptively, even in moonlight, and the flame is blurred so it is difficult to establish just where it is.'

'That's right,' Raston spoke up. He peered round guiltily. 'When I was a young man, um, well, we did some smuggling along the Medway. The best protection was the mud flats and the mist. Even on a moonlit night, you could use a lantern to good effect.'

'Aye.' Kathryn pushed the plate away. 'And I have heard stories about outlaws using lights to confuse and mislead either their victims or pursuers.'

'You get the same in the summer,' Colum explained. 'Above marshes or bogs, strange lights appear. In England, you call them Jack-o'-lanterns.'

'Very well,' Father Ealdred commented. 'But there was no evidence of anyone going down to the mere.'

'Tell me, Father,' Kathryn replied. 'If you wished to walk through a snow-covered meadow, then return with as little sign as possible, what would you do?'

162

The priest thought. 'Well, it's obvious. I'd try to follow my footprints back to the place where I started.'

'Of course,' Kathryn replied. 'And why not? You already have a path made. This will not only act as your guide but make it easier for your return as well as confuse any curious searcher.'

The priest nodded his agreement.

'Now let me ask you a second question,' Kathryn continued. 'If you were crossing that same field, covered in snow, and you saw the footprints and marks of someone else, what would you do?'

'Well, it would be easier to follow that path.'

'Which is exactly what Vavasour did.' Kathryn smiled at the old servitor. 'Raston's eyewitness account of Vavasour's death actually assisted the murderer.'

'How's that?' the old man shouted.

'It's no fault of yours,' Kathryn said. 'But the next morning, at first light, a group of people left this tavern to drag the mere for Vavasour's body. In doing so, they obliterated any sign of Vavasour's or his assassin's walk down to the mere. Kathryn stared at Tobias Smithler. 'I am correct, Master taverner?'

The landlord, his face pale and sweaty, just stared back.

Kathryn held his gaze.

'I reached my conclusions,' she explained, 'by watching a little boy play with a piece of polished wood on a frozen carp pond. That little boy, Master Smithler, trapped you.'

The landlord opened his mouth to reply but his jaw fell slack.

'I asked myself simple questions,' Kathryn continued. 'Who would know the Great Meadow?' She held a hand up. 'Oh, the other guests did, but you, Smithler, knew it very well. You know where the meadow ended and where the mere began. Secondly, who could provide a polished bowl and a heavy lantern? Who else but the landlord of the local tavern? Thirdly, who would find the footprints going across the Great Meadow the following morning? I am sure if it wasn't for Raston's intervention, it would have been you. Finally, who organized the dragging of the mere for Vavasour's corpse and, in doing so, obliterated as much evidence as possible from the Great Meadow. Of course, the answer is you.' Kathryn chewed the corner of her lip. 'I was intrigued, Master Smithler. You are not the most compassionate of men, yet you moved heaven and earth to drag the mere for this despised clerk's corpse.'

'It's true,' old Raston shouted hoarsely. 'Smithler did organise us. He was all ready, at first light. I must admit I was surprised.' He stared contemptuously at his master. 'It's the first time I sees you care anything for anybody!'

'What you did, Master taverner,' Kathryn summarised, 'was sometime before Vavasour left your tavern, you went down to the mere with a polished plate and lantern. Using a pole, you shoved the lantern across the ice as a beacon light and, of course, as a secret trap for the hapless Vavasour. That is why no tracks were left around the edge of the mere: the pole enabled you to push the light out over the ice, then turn around and follow your own tracks back to the tavern. It was a dark, freezing night. Nobody would notice you had gone. Raston was busily hunting elsewhere. Everyone else was confined to their rooms.'

'But when would Vavasour know when to leave?' Lord Alan asked. 'And would the lantern stay alight?'

'The time was prearranged,' Kathryn answered, pointing to the flickering hour candle near the hearth. 'Whilst the Smithlers, like every good citizen, possess lantern-horns that burn all night. Nobody would see it, not even Raston. Remember, he said you'd never catch rabbits in a frozen meadow. His meeting with the hapless Vavasour was purely fortuitous.'

Sir Gervase spoke up. 'But I was in the taproom when Vavasour left. Smithler was also here. Would not Vavasour have thought that was strange?' The old knight rapped the tabletop. 'And what about the coins found in Vavasour's room, eh? How can you explain them?'

'Oh, quite easily,' Kathryn replied. 'But let me take your questions one at a time. You see, when Vavasour left the taproom and walked out to the mere, he wasn't expecting to meet Master Smithler but Tobias's wife, Blanche.'

All eyes turned to where the landlord's wife sat, lips moving soundlessly; the shock of Kathryn's revelations had apparently rendered her witless.

'Mistress Smithler.' Kathryn raised her voice. 'Lady Margaret, please give her some wine.'

The noblewoman rose and went down to where the landlord's wife was sitting. She shook her gently by the shoulder. Blanche blinked, grasped the goblet of wine and, like a sleepwalker, carefully sipped from it.

'I didn't know,' the woman muttered. 'I didn't think anyone would find out.'

'Shut up!' her husband roared, reasserting himself. Smithler threw a hateful glance at Kathryn. 'You have no proof for what you say. Anyone here could have done what you describe.'

'Could they?' Colum asked. 'Shall we ask who owns a lantern and a brass or pewter plate? Or shall I gather your servants and order them to make a careful search of the tavern? I am sure one of the scullery maids will notice something is amiss.'

The landlord just glanced away.

'But the coins?' Father Ealdred insisted.

'Ah, yes, the coins,' Kathryn replied. 'Vavasour never held those coins.'

'Well, the landlord couldn't have put them there,' Standon spoke up. 'Only Vavasour had the key to his own chamber.'

'The coins were rolled under the door,' Kathryn said. 'They were put there as a diversion. You see,' she continued, 'if we had only found one coin, I could accept that Vavasour, in his haste to hide his ill-gotten gains, dropped a coin onto the rushes. He would hardly notice that. But tell me, Standon, if you were handling stolen monies in a chamber, what would you do?'

The soldier pulled a face. 'I'd lock the door,' he replied. 'And use the bed as a table.'

'Of course you would,' Kathryn agreed. 'Just to make sure you dropped nothing or left any evidence which might implicate you. Yet here's Vavasour, the cunning clerk, dropping not one coin, but several right across the chamber. Some near the fire hearth, some in the rushes and you, Master Smithler, picked one up near the wall alongside the door where few rushes lie. Now, what was Vavasour doing so close to the wall handling stolen monies? Even if he had, surely he would hear the clink as that coin hit the wooden floor? My only conclusion is that all the coins were thrown haphazardly beneath the door, each being sent in a different direction. An ill considered act,' Kathryn concluded. 'An act of desperation to divert attention to Vavasour.'

'You idiot!' Blanche Smithler had now recovered her wits; hands gripping the edge of the table, she glared across at her husband. She pointed a finger at Kathryn but she never turned to glance at her. 'You arrogant, stupid man!' Blanche hissed. 'I told you not to, but oh no, hasty as ever!'

'And Erpingham?' Lord Alan interrupted the taverner's wife. 'Mistress Swinbrooke, I accept what you say about Vavasour, but surely, the tax collector's death remains a mystery?'

Chapter 12

Let us return to the evening,' Kathryn began. 'Sir Reginald Erpingham suffered his nightmare. Sir Gervase, how did you find him?'

'Nervous, agitated, his face flushed. I think he had been retching.'

'Tell me,' Kathryn asked. 'Does anyone know what Erpingham drank or ate that night?'

'Yes,' Standon replied. 'He ordered a cup of wine from the taproom and took it upstairs, as he did on the night before he died.'

'That cup was poisoned,' Kathryn explained. 'A few grains of deadly nightshade. Not enough to kill him but enough to raise phantasms in his evil mind.'

'You mean he was drugged?' Lady Margaret asked. 'So it had nothing to do with the skull or bones found beneath the floorboards?'

'Oh no. Those are what they appear to be: a few tawdry remains, the playthings of some long-dead warlock. Now,' Kathryn continued, 'the morning after Sir Reginald's nightmare, his body was purged of any evil humours and, by the afternoon, according to all the witnesses, he was his old, wicked self. He thoroughly enjoyed being surrounded by his victims. People like yourselves who had fallen into his clutches.' Most of the guests looked away.

'Anyway, on the night the tax collector died, a special meal was cooked. Sir Reginald ate heartily, then retired for the night. He took a cup of wine upstairs and went along to his chamber. Now, what he knew, but you didn't, was that Blanche Smithler was waiting for him in his chamber.' Kathryn paused and gazed at the landlord's wife. Pale-faced but more composed, Blanche Smithler glared stony-eyed back.

'Oh yes,' Kathryn persisted. 'Why did Sir Reginald come to this tavern? Why did he bring his victims here? Why not else-where?' Kathryn coughed to clear her throat. 'To be sure, the Wicker Man served good foods, fine ales, sweet wines, but so do many other taverns in this city. Sir Reginald came here for a pur-pose. A lecherous man by nature, he was hot-eyed for Mistress Smithler. He hoped to combine seduction with business as he continued his nefarious collection of the profits of his blackmail. Erpingham stalked in here with bags heavy with silver and his lusts blazing like a furnace. He would woo Mistress Blanche, flirt, trying to grasp her body. His appetite would be whetted. After all, he was Sir Reginald, who always got his way, and why should some landlord who benefited from his custom prove any obsta-cle? However, the Smithlers had plotted his death. Now, I sus-pect, Blanche teased Sir Reginald, looking for an opportunity. What better time than when the rest of the guests and her hus-band, supposedly innocent of any knowledge of this illicit affair, had feasted and were well in their cups? Blanche agreed to meet Erpingham shortly after the banquet meal, when she had finished cooking and supervising in the kitchen. Naturally, to protect her virtue, she did not want to be seen, so she asked Erpingham to hand over the key to his chamber.'

'No, no!' Standon objected. 'Everyone was down here. Mis-tress Smithler was working in the kitchen!'

'Oh, at first she was. She would have to be. But when I asked you to recall the events of that evening, I specifically asked who went upstairs after Erpingham. I did not ask who went up before, or who came down after he had left the taproom.'

'But the taxes?' Lord Alan asked. 'Wouldn't Erpingham be wary of someone stealing them?'

'It's best if you listen,' Colum said. 'I believe Mistress Swinbrooke's account is true. Believe me, when she has finished, I intend to take this tavern apart, stick by stick and stone by stone until I find those taxes.' The Irishman chewed his lip and stared at the Smithlers. 'It stands to reason,' Colum continued, 'that the stolen taxes must be hidden here. I am sure mine host has some secret cupboard or hidden cabinet. Moreover, it would be so easy to get rid of the freshly minted silver from a tavern which buys supplies and provender, a landlord who travels around the shire purchasing this or that. Time would pass and, after a while, who could trace it back?'

Blanche Smithler abruptly pushed her chair back. Colum snapped his fingers at Standon.

'Guard her!' he ordered and, as the serjeant rose to obey, Colum nodded at Kathryn.

'On the night Erpingham died,' Kathryn said, 'you were all in the taproom eating and drinking. You had no cause to watch, or be suspicious about who went upstairs and that made it easy. Blanche Smithler would go in and out of the kitchen but, at a pre-arranged time, she would take up a water bucket, one of those standing in the gallery which had been refilled after Erpingham's room had been cleaned earlier in the day. Remember, the tax collector had been ill, his chamber and night jar would have to be washed and the bucket refilled.'

'That's right,' Raston interrupted. 'Earlier in the same day, one of the slatterns bitterly complained about the mess.'

'Mistress Smithler took it upstairs,' Kathryn explained. 'She went along the gallery with Erpingham's key in her hand and opened the door.'

'Wouldn't it creak?' Father Ealdred asked.

'No,' Kathryn replied. 'Provided you don't push them wide open, none of the doors on that gallery make a sound. Mistress Smithler is now in the chamber, but the bucket she carried is empty, at least of water; all it contains are a few rocks. She quickly empties the tax collector's saddlebag of the monies and places the rocks in. The money is put in the bucket, which, remember, is capped, probably lined with a cloth so the coins wouldn't chink.

169

She then either leaves that bucket just within the door or outside in the gallery; after all, no one is going to come along there except Erpingham. Mistress Smithler, however, also carries a goblet of wine from the new cask her husband had broached. This goblet, however, contained a deadly potion, nightshade.' Kathryn held up her hand as a sign to Sir Gervase to remain quiet.

'Now Erpingham leaves the table. He is full of good food and strong wine, and is looking forward to a tumble with the landlord's pretty wife. Upstairs he goes and taps on the door. Mistress Smithler opens it and in he goes. They would embrace. Erpingham would become excited, then Blanche would make some excuse. Some duty called, or her husband wanted her here or there, but she would return. In the excitement Erpingham had put the cup down on the table and, besotted with lust, doesn't realise that Mistress Smithler has changed hers for his. She pretends to be equally desirous and swears she will return. She tells him to be ready. She picks up the untainted wine goblet and her bucket and slips out of the room. She goes along the gallery to her own chamber, around the corner. She hides the bucket there, picks up an identical one, puts it on the gallery and then returns downstairs.'

'The rest of you,' Colum added, 'were still finishing your wine. Master Smithler would have kept you busy until his wife's return.'

'A very short time,' Kathryn observed. 'I calculate no more than ten minutes from the time Sir Reginald left the table.'

'But, Mistress,' Sir Gervase said. 'I accept what you say. But wouldn't Erpingham check his taxes?'

'Oh, it was a gamble,' Kathryn replied. 'But even if he had, how could he blame Mistress Smithler? No, we must see matters through the dead man's eyes. He is there in his chamber, flushed with drink and full of lust. He cannot wait for Mistress Smithler's return. He undresses, throwing his clothes on the floor and dons his nightshirt. Perhaps he did look at the saddlebags, but they were heavy and bulky, properly strapped down. He barely gives them a second thought, the only thing on his mind being Mistress Smithler.' Kathryn paused and sipped from her wine cup. She smiled at Lord Alan. 'Tell me, sir, if you were in a similar situation, and I only say if, and you have a goblet of wine, what would you do?'

The nobleman grinned. 'I'd gulp it fast.'

'Aye,' Kathryn said. 'And Erpingham did the same, not knowing he was drinking his own death. If he felt strange, he'd have put it down to the meal, the wine, the heavy excitement. Standon came along the gallery but Erpingham dismissed him.' Kathryn smoothed the tabletop with her fingers. 'Only then does he feel ill. He lies down on the bed.' She shrugged. 'The deadly nightshade has its effect.' She sighed. 'The rest you know. The next morning Standon goes upstairs. Erpingham, of course, cannot be roused, so the door is forced.'

'But the wine cup!' Father Ealdred exclaimed. 'The wine in the cup in Erpingham's chamber was not tainted!'

Kathryn was about to reply when there was a furious knocking on the door.

'Everyone stay!' Colum ordered.

He went down the passageway, past the kitchen where the servants clustered fearfully together. Colum realised they must have overheard what was going on. He unlocked the door of the tavern and blinked at the strong light from the lanterns Luberon and the city bailiff were carrying. Colum smiled and beckoned them in.

'Master Luberon, just in time.'

Luberon pulled back the cowl of his hood and grasped Colum by the arm. 'Mistress Swinbrooke has trapped him?'

Colum drew his head back in mock surprise. 'What do you mean, Simon?'

'She has!' Luberon smacked his gloved hands together. 'I knew it, as soon as I received her message.' He pushed Colum along the corridor. 'Who is it? Who is it?'

'Shush!' Colum held a hand up and handed the keys to the bailiff. 'Lock and guard the door!' he ordered. 'The rest of you stay at the entrance to the taproom.' He beckoned Luberon forward. 'The Smithlers,' Colum whispered.

Luberon stopped. 'It can't be!' he exclaimed. 'It can't be!'

'Why not?'

Luberon blew his cheeks out as he unclasped his cloak.

'This time,' he smiled apologetically, 'I thought I would do some searching of my own. The city is silent so I sent a number of pursuivants round the city apothecaries. You know, those who sell the occasional noxious potion or sleeping draught. One of our guests here bought some, only a few grains.'

'Who?' Colum asked.

Luberon slipped him a piece of parchment. 'You'd best give that to Mistress Kathryn.'

Colum and Luberon returned to the taproom. Luberon pulled up a chair to sit at the other side of Kathryn. Colum whispered in Kathryn's ear and handed her the piece of parchment the clerk had given to her. Kathryn stared down at the name and blinked in astonishment.

'What about the wine?' Father Ealdred asked, ignoring Luberon's entrance. 'The wine in the cup taken from the chamber the morning Erpingham was found dead. It was untainted.'

'Yes, yes, it was,' Kathryn replied absent-mindedly. 'But that was quite simple. Master Luberon, your arrival is fortuitous. I believe you were called to the Wicker Man the morning Erpingham was found dead?'

'Oh yes, yes, I was!'

'And Standon, you were on guard?'

The serjeant nodded.

'And the landlord entered the dead man's chamber?'

'Yes, I told you that: he came in to view the corpse like the rest. Ah!' the soldier sneered. 'I follow your thread, Mistress.'

'Smithler carried a goblet under his cloak or in his pouch,' Kathryn explained. 'An identical goblet with some wine dregs in it. The cups were quietly changed and the mystery was posed.'

'But why kill Vavasour?' Luberon asked.

'Well,' Kathryn said and grinned, 'like many other clerks I know, Vavasour had a nose for mischief and an enquiring mind. Now, on my first visit here, when I came down to question all the guests, I brought the wine cup left in Erpingham's chamber. Vavasour was sharp-eyed. He'd been sitting next to his master that night. Perhaps he noticed the difference, a crack, a mark in the cup or stem. So, he began to piece the puzzle together. Remember, Vavasour also knew his master's weakness: Erpingham loved seductions. Vavasour reached the same conclusion I did, hence his oft-quoted quip, 'There's many a slip 'twixt cup and lip.' Vavasour was enigmatically referring to the fact that he had discovered his master's cup had been changed. The only persons who could have done this were the Smithlers.' Kathryn pointed down at Blanche. 'Despite your cold-blooded ruthlessness, Mistress, you have a pretty face. Vavasour should have recalled another proverb: 'Don't judge a book by its cover', but he did, and made a terrible mistake. If Mistress Smithler had been prepared to sleep with his master, only she was involved.'

Kathryn played with her wine cup. She glanced sharply at the person named in Luberon's scrap of parchment and realised she had made one error. She only hoped she had not made others.

'Vavasour approached Mistress Smithler,' Kathryn continued. 'She, of course, acted all frightened. She explained she could not meet him in the tavern and so that fateful meeting on the mere was arranged. Vavasour would not realise he had been trapped. The night he left the tavern, he probably checked who was still there and found Tobias Smithler busy in the taproom so, being Erpingham's clerk, eager for profits and confident that Blanche would pose no serious problem, he went out to meet her. Vavasour was expecting a quick profit, half, perhaps even more, of the stolen taxes. After all, Erpingham was dead and Vavasour recognized his days of thievery were over forever. In the end, the Smithlers also killed him and, in a moment of panic, rolled those coins beneath the door so as to incriminate Vavasour even further.'

'What Vavasour didn't know,' Colum intervened, 'is that, perhaps half an hour earlier, Tobias Smithler had taken the lantern down to the mere and set his trap.'

'The same time,' Raston bitterly observed, 'they knew that I, the only person who'd be out on such a night, was busy elsewhere.'

'In his greedy desire for a quick profit,' Kathryn declared, 'Vavasour would go anywhere for such a fortune and, not being a local man, forgot about the mere, as he did about the thaw.'

'You sharp-eyed bitch!' Blanche Smithler hissed. 'And, before you ask'—she sneered contemptuously at her husband who now sat dejectedly—'the idea was mine. Erpingham came here to paw me. He once tried to drag me into the stables to ruffle my petticoats. I couldn't stand his stink, yet every time he became more importunate. He was a wicked, evil man. He deserved his death.' She started to rise but Standon forced her back in the chair.

'So sharp,' she taunted Kathryn. 'One day, Mistress, you'll cut yourself. But you got two things wrong. First, I never poisoned Erpingham's goblet the night that evil bastard suffered his nightmare. Like you, my good physician, I know poisons. If I had meant to kill Erpingham, I would have done.'

'And the second matter?' Colum asked.

Blanche Smithler pointed to her husband. 'He thinks we are finished, but I know different. Who cares whether an evil tax collector has received his just deserts? Or that little demon Vavasour? Who will weep for them? The King's Exchequer in London?'

'The taxes?' Colum asked softly.

'Oh yes.' She sneered. 'The King's precious taxes, worth much more than you think, Irishman. Those coins are freshly minted; on the bullion market they'll fetch a high price. Now . . .' She leaned her arms on the table.

Colum held his hand up for silence.

'The rest of you can leave,' he ordered. 'Wait in your chambers until this matter is finished. You, too, Master Standon. Luberon's bailiffs will keep us secure.'

The guests were only too eager to scrape back their chairs and flee the taproom.

'What is going to happen, Irishman?' Kathryn whispered.

'She is going to bargain for her life and I think we'll have to accept it.'

Once the room was cleared Colum gestured at the Smithlers.

'Well, the taxes?'

'You can tear this tavern apart,' Blanche declared. 'Stick by stick, stone by stone' was the phrase you used. Well, do so. I promise you, Irishman, I may well hang on the city scaffold and my corpse and that of my husband be gibbeted at some lonely crossroads but the King's taxes will never be found. And what will you do then, Irishman? What will you, or your snivelling clerk, write to the golden-haired Edward?'

Tobias Smithler also raised his head and grinned weakly at his wife, who sat rigid as a piece of steel, red spots of anger high in her pale, pretty face.

'You know what I want, Irishman. Our lives: the King's taxes in return for our life and liberty.' She gestured round the tavern. 'Oh, I know we are felons. All our goods are escheated to the King. So, how will the Crown suffer? The death of a corrupt tax collector, the murder of a miserable clerk? But, if the King gets his monies and the profits of this tavern, who loses then, eh?'

Kathryn shivered at Blanche's cold, calculating offer.

'You killed two human beings,' Kathryn replied. 'You took away their lives. Erpingham may have been evil, and Vavasour corrupt, but their lives were a matter between them and God, not just the playthings of your greed.'

'Oh, shut up!' Blanche snapped. 'You hoity-toity physician with your sense of righteousness!'

'I am neither,' Kathryn retorted. 'As I am no assassin.'

Blanche spread her hands. 'Then let the King's Justice have his way. Irishman, load me with chains, send us down to Newgate in London to stand trial before the King's Bench. Two more deaths will occur but where are the King's taxes, eh?'

Colum grasped Kathryn's arm. He pushed his face close to hers. Luberon leaned across to listen.

'She's a wicked woman,' Colum murmured. 'But she has the truth of it. They have hidden the monies and the King will be furious. God knows what might happen. Everyone in this tavern could be held accountable for these monies and that includes us. There again, the barons of the Exchequer may simply rule that no taxes were delivered so no taxes were collected and the people of these parts will pay twice.'

'They'll be pardoned?' Kathryn whispered.

'Oh, no.' Colum looked at Blanche Smithler. 'Woman, you have my word as the King's Commissioner.' He pulled out a cross on a piece of cord that hung round his neck. 'I swear, if you return those taxes, you'll have your lives.'

'For how long?' Tobias Smithler asked.

'I don't play games with murderers,' Colum replied, still clasping the cross. 'Bring the monies down here. There are scales in the kitchen. Master Luberon will weigh it and check that all is well.'

'And then what?'

'You will go as you are,' Colum replied, 'to the sanctuary church of St. Mary in Queningate. You will claim sanctuary and remain there, untroubled, for forty days. If the Exchequer concludes that every penny Erpingham collected has been returned, you will, towards the end of January, be allowed to leave that church and take the road to Dover. You will take no provisions, no staff, no property. You will be furnished with a cross. You will not be allowed to leave the King's highway. At the King's port of Dover, you must throw yourselves upon the mercy of any sea captain. You will leave England, and all territories under the jurisdiction of the Crown, never to return on pain of death!'

Blanche Smithler's face lost some of its hardness. 'You are a ruthless man, Irishman.'

'And you are very fortunate,' Colum retorted. 'Now, I will sit back and count to one hundred. If those taxes are not returned by the time I finish, you will hang. Mistress Smithler, stay with us, your husband will find what we are all looking for.'

The landlord fairly leapt from his seat and ran upstairs.

'Do we have to keep our word?' Luberon whispered.

Colum stared up at the blackened rafters. 'This tavern has stood here for centuries. God knows what secret cupboards and closets exist.' He looked bleakly across at the clerk. 'The King will be pleased. Erpingham and Vavasour were corrupt: he will seize all their property. He also has his taxes back, not to mention a comfortable tavern.'

'You are not counting, Irishman!' Blanche Smithler said.

Colum spread his hands and grinned. 'What's the use?' he replied. 'Once I get past fifty I'm in difficulties. I am sure your husband has my meaning.'

His words were greeted by a pounding on the stairs and Smithler, breathing heavily, came into the room carrying two bulky sacks and slammed them down on the table.

Colum snapped his fingers at one of the bailiffs.

'You and three of your men take the landlord and his wife down to Queningate. They may take cloaks and suitable footwear.'

'And food?' Smithler wailed.

'Whatever you can quickly collect from the buttery,' Colum added.

Kathryn sat and watched the prisoners, surrounded by the bailiffs, go into the kitchen and return. Each carried a small linen bundle. The bailiffs paused at the foot of the stairs whilst the Smithlers went up to their chamber. Once they were down, they were hustled towards the door. Blanche Smithler suddenly turned. Kathryn steeled herself at the look of pure hatred in the woman's dark eyes.

'I'll go!' Blanche rasped. 'I'll go to the church and, in forty days, I will be free of Canterbury!' She pointed a finger at Kathryn. 'But never forget me, Swinbrooke, because, before God, I shall never forget you!'

The bailiffs dragged her away, down the passageway; the door to the tavern was unlocked, then slammed shut behind them. Kathryn stared at the money bags.

'Two men died for those,' she murmured. She glanced at Luberon. 'Well, Simon, you are the city clerk. I suggest you have them weighed, numbered and counted, then placed in the guildhall strong box. When the roads are clear, they can be sent to their owners in London.'

Luberon, licking his lips, picked up the heavy bags and staggered into the kitchen. Kathryn stared into the dying fire. She rose and took a log from the pile heaped on the hearth, threw it on, then stood warming her fingers. Colum came up behind her. He grasped her shoulders and kissed her gently on the back of the head.

'Physician, you did well.'

Kathryn looked over her shoulder. ' "Thus ends the third part, so begins the fourth and last part," as The Knight's Tale puts it.'

'What do you mean, Kathryn?' Colum turned her around and stared into her tear-filled eyes. 'Kathryn, what's the matter?'

She shivered. 'I don't know.' She chewed on her lip. 'God save us, Colum, did you see the hate in that woman's eyes?'

The Irishman shrugged. 'A wicked woman, frustrated in her ways.'

'No.' Kathryn shook her head and stared across the darkened taproom. 'Before God, Colum,' she whispered, 'I have yet to see the last of Blanche Smithler.'

'Empty words,' Colum scoffed. 'She'll be lucky to reach Dover alive.' He grasped Kathryn's cold hands and squeezed them. 'And you will always have me.'

Kathryn cocked her head slightly, listening to Luberon singing in the kitchen as he merrily counted the coins.

'Is it all there, Simon?'

'Oh, yes,' he shouted back. 'As Master Murtagh is fond of quoting, "*Avaritia radix malorum:* The love of money is truly the root of all evil." I could kill for this myself!'

'I don't think so!' Kathryn replied.

Luberon went on singing. Kathryn smiled at Colum and turned back to the fire.

'We are not finished yet.' She unrolled the scrap of parchment in her hand. 'We need to see Father Ealdred. Please, Colum, bring him down. I'll explain then.'

The Irishman left and returned a few minutes later with the priest. Kathryn threw the scrap of parchment onto the fire and turned to greet him.

'Father, I'll come swiftly to the point. Did you intend to kill Sir Reginald Erpingham? Is that why Standon heard you mutter "Too much! Too much!"?'

Ealdred's face paled. 'Before God, Mistress,' he whispered, 'I don't know. In my parish I am a herbalist, not a physician like yourself but, after Erpingham's visit, I seethed with rage. I was tired of his wickedness and the way he abused poor women.' He ran a finger round the collar of his shirt. 'I was so tired of Erpingham. I didn't want to kill him, but as I passed through the city, I stopped at an apothecary's and bought a small dose of deadly nightshade. On the evening before he had the nightmare, Smithler passed me Erpingham's goblet of wine. I put a few grains in. If I had really wanted to, I could have killed him, but I knew his sleep would be disturbed. I thought it might be a warning. I'd taken him aside and pleaded with him but he'd laughed, so I was pleased when I heard how frightened he had been. I intended to speak to him later, claim it was a warning from God.' He smiled thinly at Kathryn. 'But, apparently, God intervened before I could.' The priest took a step closer to Kathryn. 'I did not want Erpingham dead,' he pleaded. 'Punished, yes.'

Kathryn picked up her cloak from where it lay over a stool. She swung it round her and smiled at the priest.

'Well, you can tell the rest, Father, it's finished. God's justice has been done and so has the King's. Never again will Sir Reginald Erpingham visit your village and harass and abuse members of your parish.'

She left the passageway, Colum followed her.

'Sir! Sir!' Raston came hurrying along behind. 'What will happen to the tavern?'

'Why, Master Raston,' Colum replied, ''till the King decides, you manage it.' He clasped the old man's hands. 'Be careful when you go poaching, especially on these cold, dark nights. I shall mention the service you gave, so you must live long enough to enjoy your reward.'

He and Kathryn bade farewell to Luberon and went out into the freezing night. They pulled up the cowls of their cloaks, hiding their faces behind their mufflers. Colum linked his arm through Kathryn's. Once they were clear of the tavern, back on the alleyway leading into the city, Kathryn paused and stared up at the brilliant night sky.

'What do you think, Irishman? Will it snow before Christmas?'

Colum pulled a face. 'Now in Ireland we have a saying: If it snows before Christmas it will be a long, hard winter. Whatever it does, Kathryn, let's enjoy the feast.'

'Not half as much as Wuf will his marzipan tomorrow,' Kathryn murmured.

'Aye,' Colum sighed. 'He's a good lad. He can come out with me to Kingsmead.' He glanced at Kathryn. 'You did well.'

'Perhaps,' she replied. 'But could it all have been avoided? If Alisoun Blunt had been a good and honourable wife? If the Smithlers hadn't been so avaricious and Erpingham so wicked?'

'To quote the Pardoner,' Colum began, 'The devil found them in such a wicked state, he had full leave his rage to consummate.'

Kathryn laughed and, clutching his arm, walked on.

'I've just decided, Irishman, what to buy you for Christmas.'

'Which is?'

Kathryn grinned mischievously. 'Something to help you count past fifty!'

Author's Note

The use of hallucinogenic drugs in the Middle Ages was quite common and the strange effect of nightshade and other herbal concoctions was carefully noted. Many writers now agree that the visions of so-called witches were linked to these drugs. Indeed the word 'assassin' is a corruption of the word 'hashish', the opiate eaten by members of an eleventh-century Syrian sect before they carried out their drug-induced crimes.

Tax collectors, at least in Medieval England, were usually hated and their nefarious practices were a constant complaint by Parliament. Time and again, they were attacked, physically as well as verbally, and their depredations were a constant factor in peasant uprisings, especially in the fifteenth and sixteenth centuries.

A word about the dialogue and characters: certain modern concepts and idioms separate us from the fifteenth century, but a survey of Margaret Paston's letters (died 1484) show emotions and their expression not very different from our own. Indeed, I used Margaret Paston as a model for Kathryn Swinbrooke: industrious, composed, single-minded and committed to a world of work. Women such as Margaret Paston were models of propriety in an age where emotional outbursts or sexual impropriety by a woman could mean public and private disgrace. Chivalry and the language of the Courts of Love may sound very pleasant to our modern ears; to the women of the fifteenth century however, they were simply a pleasant diversion from the grim struggle against war, pestilence, superstition and sudden death.